Katherine N. Gorman

D0897542

The Little Book of Baby/Child

Influence glial cells (the other 90% of brain cells), choose good genetics, create optimum health and intelligence, and secure the emotional well-being, of your growing child.

Author: Katherine N. Gorman

e-mail: kateaset@gmail.com

Published by: MG&5, LLC
160 Saddlebrook Path
Southington, CT 06489
e-mail:mgandfive@gmail.com

Library of Congress Control Number: 2016903277

ISBN # 978-0-9907813-8-7

There's a girl in the world with a peanut butter swirl on the top of her only curl. She twirls and she twirls and she twirls and she twirls, singing …
I'm gonna change the world!

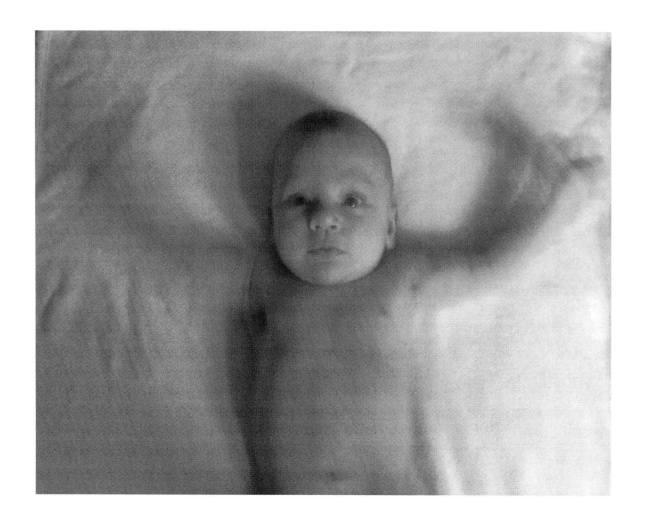

I want to deeply and sincerely thank my daughter, who is a courageous, beautiful and strong being. The sheer force of her nature brought me to the knowledge written here. Without her, this book would not be. You got wings baby!

CONTENTS

Introduction

PART I: THE ENVIRONMENT OF EARLY CHILDHOOD

PART II: EMOTIONS and HEALING THEM

INTRODUCTION:

Let me introduce myself. I am Kate Gorman, the author of this book, my seven year-old daughter ... the book's illumination. Meaning most everything I share with you inside this experience is somehow connected to her spirit, creativity and life direction. I (which includes my daughter) hope to walk with you, laugh with you and think with you, inside pregnancy, birth and child-raising (conception is respected as a private matter). I, not so secretly hope that there will be a big impact, something we (the "we" strongly includes, and is, YOU) make together, like a generation changed. With that said, I need to begin with a little warning: Sometimes I use off-colored, inappropriate humor, the kind of things a Licensed Clinical Social Worker aught not say. I really don't say these things to my clients, but I feel that you can handle it. Not that my clients can't handle it, but in sessions I am bound by the rules of my profession (shhh, for the most part). See, I'm kidding again. Anyway, I hope that my jokes go over well, and you are therefore less bored by my writing. If at any point I offend you, you can throw the book on the floor and say, "I can't believe she said that," and then forgive me, pick it back up again, knowing that I really only wanted to make you laugh.

OK, now we can go on. When I became pregnant with my daughter some eight years ago, I felt an imperative (a very, very strong one), to maintain the original light this being was created from, unclouded by genetic history, trauma, toxins and programming that humans are daily faced with (good luck right?!). This imperative launched me on an information-hunting, stop-at-nothing sort of path. While pregnancy hormones might have something to do with my quest, I will venture to say, that I was getting a soulful push from the being, soon to be born. Nevertheless, I researched and talked with practitioners, healers, shamans, midwives, mothers and fathers (the push, the quest and the people/practitioner researching continues and greatly informs the book).

So, my pregnancy was guided by research and by instincts which, by the way, are never as crystal clear as when you're pregnant. This book is, in part, about listening to them! I refused to hear anything other than those instincts (well, 75 % of the time), even when I doubted. The voice inside me (which is hooked up to my very large, personal team of Archangels) said, "you are having a girl, everything is going to be fine, and you need do nothing related to typical standard care." So, I had no OBGYN, and for the most part, my care included a baby daddy and a midwife. Uh ... people don't like this very much, and want to convey their learned fears about pregnancy as an illness. All I can say is, don't let them. I would like to very sincerely thank my sister Jennifer Wisner, who is a courageous forerunner in the world and was a forerunner in all of this for me. To the last day before birth, she was the cheerleader of my choices. **Note:** The baby daddy and I are now divorced, which is a story for masochists and not for your wonderful ears. However, I will say that the baby daddy also aligned with my choices (I guess that would make it our choices), without question and in total support. I am grateful to him for that.

Now the standard care thing ... which I did none of, is not something I am against. Really, I am not against it. What I am for, is a woman's connection to her instinct, undisturbed by some intellectual system that sometimes, not always, tell her she's wrong. What I am for is more knowledge about "what the heck" is going on in those systems that dictate the natural rhythms of birth and health (for profit). Oh God (I mean this in an invoking way, not in vain), did I just say that out loud? I am now pulling down the shades.

OK, um, nothing happened. We are really so blessed to make our own choices (and say potentially unpopular things … love that right to free speech) without repercussions in America. So anyway, what I gained along the way (about not choosing standard care choices) I realized, is not commonly known and this book is because, I believe, it needs to be. *The Little Book of Baby/Child's* intention is to give families more choices, more understanding and more decision-making power. May it be that for you. **Note:** Remember these are our bodies and our children's bodies, we govern them, we decide. This is not an "f you" or "kiss my ass" western medicine, this is "I appreciate you" and "I love you" and "please listen to me" western medicine. **Double note (or disclaimer):** I am your idea girl, not your diagnosis girl, so if you need to go to the western med. doc., please go! You know what I mean broken arms, high fevers or strange rashes … you gotta go!

Anyhow … it's important for us to hold together (no matter what) … we live connected as parents for the next generation. We need each other. Know that I honor that maybe three or four recommendations from this book may work for you and the rest may not. There are so many things to consider in all different types of families, work situations, major stresses and lifestyles. There is no judgment. (Well maybe a little judgment {kidding}, but I still love you.) Even as you hear the passion I have about certain topics, I will honor and trust you when you decide differently from what I recommend. I am sure that if I walked in your shoes, I might make the same choice and … there are no wrong answers, when your gut is being heard by you. *Here's my recommended formula …* **Gut + Research = Highest and Best Decision.** Not recommended formula … What your mother-in-law would do + Pressure from a closed-minded physician = Lame Decision (unless your mother-in-law is really awesome and religiously watched Oprah to learn about all different holistic, traditional and spiritual practices, informing her open-minded recommendation to you, and, most importantly, your gut tells you to agree with her).

What is written inside this book comes from a belief that every woman and every man, is progressing evolution, and, I think there are faster ways to do so. I have learned that there are ways to get the body to choose the best genetics. These codes of life are not just subject to natural selection as we once thought. These codes are influenced by trauma, toxins, by the environment, by thought, by emotions and by food. ***This book weaves information about the other 90% of the brain cells, the glial cells, and their very important role in that best genetic expression, as well as glia communication with the blood-brain barrier.*** (**Side note:** The glia cells can be programmed by our thoughts and in the later sections we talk about our emotions, patterns and reprogramming the brain.) There is so much information available for us today about how to influence the very molecules which make up good health. Listen to your baby/child and to your own instincts, as you research what is best for you, your child and your family. This book is a spark … *The Little Book of Baby/Child,* search items included.

Special note: We touch on topics like structure, education and spirituality. We are also going to get to some more challenging subjects like ultrasounds, vaccines and child body boundary issues. Remember let's hold together, keep making jokes and keep our eye on solutions for everyone.

We are holding hands, don't let go.

Special admit: Well, I … I hope you're not too mad at me, but I named the book *The Little Book of Baby/Child*, mostly because I wanted everyone to find it on a Google search (you know child, baby and book … all pretty universal). I could have named it *"How to Get Your Baby to Walk on Water?"* or *"How to Make a Baby Earth Steward?"* but I thought I would narrow my reading population to Christians or hippies. Though I really love both populations, I really want everyone to find the information. So while it may seem to be a marketing scheme, it is really an intention to secure life into its finest form, within as many families as possible. Wow, did you just hear me … "secure life into its finest form" don't I have a lot of nerve? All that and a bag of chips (only organic of course!). Oh and as for little in the title, the book was supposed to be so little, you could use staples to seam the pages together. I had an intention to crank something out in a couple of months, almost a pamphlet that I envisioned at every baby doctor's office … two and half years later and a much bigger book! Now it is just … sort of little or, little in comparison to some.

*****Oh, before we go on … the Baby Daddy gets credit for the sperm of course, and for all photos used within the book. Thank you Baby Daddy.

Special thanks: Although my daughter, God Bless her, has truly been my greatest teacher, I've also been schooled in my work as a psychotherapist. I have met many extraordinary families and people making extraordinary decisions, each different and valuable. I have worked with extraordinary providers who are taking huge leaps in treating children and people holistically. I am very grateful to all of them (the families and the providers that is).

I want to thank newborn specialist Lindsay Gibson, who provided important insight into hospital births and procedures for the book. I am so grateful for her dedication to empowering women and for making newborns very important people. Thank you to Jeanette Dias, a lovely, powerful artist of the world and dear friend, who has inspired so much in this process. I want to thank Dr. Diana Lopusny and Nicole Casbarro, APRN, who are courageous pioneers in holistic pediatric health! Thank you for guidance and information, friendship and support. Dr. Lopusny also gets big high fives and an extra dose of gratitude for her contribution to the nutrition and health section of the book. Side **Note:** Dr. superstar Lopusny is working to open a school called Treetop Landing, whose mission is to provide an affordable, creative, inventive and progressive environment of child-directed learning. (Please check out www.treetoplanding.org and consider making a donation to this really important cause. There is an easy PayPal thing, please donate even five bucks or $100,000 if you are super wealthy. With a portion of the proceeds from this book, I will also do the PayPal thing.)

Deep thank you and I love you to Cindy, TJ, Jon, Jen, Rob, Debbie (sometimes referred to as my daughter's Waddy - woman daddy), Lisa, Ralph, my parents Cath and Mike Gorman, family and friends who have held me up and have been those people in my daughter's life that build resilience (I may have had … a few tiny years, when I was a train wreck). Thank you again, to my parents, for all your good parenting, love, prayers and all those extra fifty dollar occasions when my account was at negative $12.

Another thank you to my sweet and intelligent mama for editing the book for me (and for giving me life!), along with my sweet and intelligent Aunt Lynn, who caught all the little mistakes we missed. Then when they were done, I added another fifty pages to the book and so I thank the vibrant, love-emanating Carolann Asselin, who then edited the additions. (If you find mistakes in the book, it is not their fault … I kept adding. I tend to over comma the heck out of things, wanting lots of pause. I also take artistic liberties with grammar on occasion. Forgive me.)

To my very dear-to-me father, to whom I owe countless points of gratitude, thank you for publishing this book (and for lending me your computer in those final weeks into months of writing!).

Lastly, I want to thank my sister Cindy Burnett for all her help and encouragement, but especially, for the design of the book's cover. She is the gal with the metaphorical pick-up truck of graphic design with lots of folks asking her to move their creative projects. She is brilliant, generous and sincerely helped raise me (well into adulthood). Love you Sista!

PART I: THE ENVIRONMENT OF EARLY CHILDHOOD

1. GLIAL CELLS, the other 90% of the brain:

For some time, I had been asking (no one in particular) why or how thought/emotion could make health or disease. I think it may have been my team of Archangels that answered me. In 2011, my two year-old and I strolled into Barnes & Noble and there it was! Scientific America, Douglas Fields and the Glial cells (Glial cells control synaptic connections to neurons, the production of neurotransmitters and communication for hormone production). Essentially, glial cells control all neuro-functions through to the ENTIRE central nervous system, and thought moves the action of the glial cells (Koob, 2009)! (Sincere special thanks to Douglas Fields and Andrew Koob for your glial cell research.) This light bulb, holy cow moment, was found in the children's section of a chain bookstore, with mothers flipping through Vogue magazines sipping their Starbucks. My own Vogue was just waiting for me to finish solving the answer to my big question so I could get my style on. Just an unrelated fact, I love Starbucks coffee (yes, mostly decaf while breastfeeding), though I'd like them to brew organic ... pretty please! **Note:** This is the point (2011) when I really get going with my talks to lots of doctors, neuroscientists, naturopaths and so on. My father, who is truly the greatest of men, often met me in places all of over Connecticut to watch my daughter while I plugged my take on reprogramming the glial cells (see later sections on brain reprogramming) to whatever provider would agree to listen to me.

So anyway, the glial cells are the other ninety percent of the brain cells. We have been told that we only use ten percent of our brain (neurons), so if I do the math, looks we could get to one hundred percent use. In the past ten or so years, neuroscience has been shifting its' focus from neurons to glia and all the latest research supports glia as the captain cell. The higher up the evolutionary ladder the more glial cells there are, with dolphins and whales having the most, and humans, not too far behind (Koob, 2009). The only difference in Einstein's brain (I think it is preserved somewhere), when compared to normal human brains is ... you guessed it, more glial cells! (Koob, 2009). Emotions and feelings, cycles of attention, cognitive changes and the acquisition of skills, are reliant upon the communication of glia and their control over synapses, the release of neurotransmitters, as well as the function of neurons (Fields, 2010). **Note:** While I am not a fan of animal testing, human glia grafted into tiny cute lab mice made for smarter tiny cute lab mice in behavioral learning and memory tasks, when compared to their not so mighty mouse peers (Han et al., 2013). Thank you tiny lab mice for your contribution to the world!

So ... here's a super quick informational about the glia. I hope it makes an easy reference as we look at how thought, life choices and the environment interacts with the function and growth of these very, very, very important cells.

How do glial cells communicate? Glial cells communicate to each other via calcium waves (Cornell-Bell, 1990) much like cell phones, sending messages through the brain and then on to the body. What you think initiates the waves!!!!

What do glial cells do? The star-shaped glial cells, called astrocytes, are the most prevalent of these awesome cells and act as your motherboard. "Motherboard," meaning that these cells are located in the pre-frontal cortex (where thought originates) and are in control of the messages sent through the brain and then onto the body (Koob, 2009). The astrocytes instruct the connection of synapses on your fast train, the neurons. In fact one human astrocyte can influence two million synapses (Fields, Douglas, 2010). If there is an instruction to connect, "I am a horrible person," then all systems run connections to this program. I recommend the replacement program of "I am a beautiful, superstar genius," unless you are legitimately horrible then you have to face this and possibly go to therapy to correct your bad behavior. Most of us are running programs that aren't true, and you really don't want to run them in your child. When the astrocytes are working well, essentially everything in the body is working well (Gosselin et al., 2010). *When astrocytes are activated by ill-thought, stress, emotions, toxins, food and even radiation from our cell phones, they could theoretically switch their function (from resting to activated) and when astrocytes are activated there is a greater chance of unhealthy gene expression* (Gosselin et al., 2010).

Gamma Oscillations in higher level brain function: Astrocytes have a strong role in gamma oscillations … waves of brain activity associated with memory, creativity and learning (Lee, H. et al., 2014).

Glial Cells and this book: There are all kinds of glial cells with all kinds of important functions (sorry not to name them all here), but please remember the astrocytes … essentially the control panel of our brain and bodies. This book's purpose is to give the best chance at happy astrocytes in your baby and child and, with hope, healthy genes are then chosen. So much affects this early development, which affects every aspect of the life that follows. What you choose now will support the essential nature of your child into adulthood.

Special note about the PLACEBO EFFECT: I hypothesize that glial cells are responsible for the placebo effect: belief changing physiology. I hope to show you how you can best influence positive communication of glia (belief or calcium wave direction) for best physical development (physiology or good girl/good boy glial cells follow instruction to make change). **Side note on special note:** Chances are good that someone with a vast amount of neuroscience experience and possibly a Nobel peace prize has this hypothesis published in some fancy German medical journal (the Germans are a bit ahead of us in medicine). However, I haven't found much out there to this "glial cell responsible for placebo effect" regard.

Brief note before the next section: The next segments are focused on conception, pregnancy and birth. If you are reading this and have already birthed your baby, please read on anyway. The birthing information segments can help you to understand the function of the glial cells and the blood-brain barrier. Even if you have done none of what has been recommended, it's just fine. Glial cells can reproduce new glial cells and I believe that anything that you wanted to do differently can be rewritten in the brain (see last sections on programming the brain).

Before we get into all the good stuff, one more brief section on some brain functions. Stay with me, we will connect it all and you rock!

2. PINEAL GLAND and THE BLOOD-BRAIN BARRIER:

Third eye: The pineal gland is a small endocrine gland located in the center of the brain which regulates sleep, temperature and along with your regular eyes, assists in the integration of light in the body. Both your eyes and pineal gland contain photoreceptor cells that relate to circadian rhythms. Perhaps that's why many spiritual traditions consider the pineal gland to be the "third eye" for its "sight"… the ability to see pictures, dreams and visions in the inside of our mind. Needless to say, it is an important gland and you will be sent back here for review (if you want to) in a few of the upcoming sections.

The National Institute of Health (NIH) presented the article, *Gene Scan Shows Body's Clock Influences Numerous Physical Functions: From Immunity to Thyroid Hormones, Pineal Gland Exerts Effects on 600 Genes:* Researchers found that the pineal gland has important influence over genetics that control inflammation, the immune response, cell adhesion, reproduction and death of cells, calcium metabolism, cholesterol production, **endothelial cells** (in blood vessels) and endothelial tissue (the tissue that lines body's organs), cytoskeleton (the inner structural material of cells), transcription (the process by which DNA sequences are converted in proteins), effects on the thyroid gland, cell signaling and hormones and copper and zinc biology (www.nih.gov/news-events/news-releases/gene-scan-shows-bodys-clock-influences-numerous-physical-functions, 2009).

In summation, this gland is pretty important!

You may have noticed that I randomly bolded **endothelial cells** in the last paragraph. Great noticing! **Endothelial cells** are the central component of the blood-brain barrier. The blood-brain barrier is the restraint mechanisms of cell junctions, between the blood and cerebrospinal fluid (CSF) (Sanders et al., 2012). Essentially, it is the wall that keeps unwanted molecules away, from the most important parts of the brain's functioning. **Think important cells that form a wall to protect.**

Next, consider that endothelial cells are controlled by your master cells the astrocytes (Alvarez, J., Katayama, T. and Prat, A., 2013) and influenced by the pineal gland as said above. So after being mothered by the pineal gland, the endothelial cells follow the master, the astrocytes, in keeping a strong blood-brain barrier. The pineal gland and astrocytes are on the phone with each other talking about a lot of processes, but certainly about the behavior of the darling endothelial cells. But, if the astrocytes get upset (from stress, trauma, toxins) they may communicate like a woman whose birthday was forgotten and her friends (endothelial cells and pineal gland) feel a little lost wondering what's going on. Really it is not that astrocytes are sulking, they become very busy working out problems in whatever they are encountering in stress and strain, leaving the endothelial cells somewhat vulnerable (Alvarez, J., Katayama, T. and Prat, A., 2013). In newborns, infants and toddlers the blood brain barrier, is already vulnerable … In the article *Barrier Mechanism in Developing Brains*, it described the infant blood-brain barrier as "leaky." This "may render developing brains more vulnerable to drugs, toxins, and pathological conditions, contributing to cerebral damage, and later neurological disorders" (Sanders et. al,

12

2012).

Standard care could be interfering with these brain functions: Ok, what I am trying to say here is that an embryo has an underdeveloped blood-brain barrier, so does an infant, toddler and so on (hopefully strengthening with age). Many standard care procedures (ultrasounds, induction, birth procedures, possible shock from pain of vaccinations, toxic shock from vaccines) could create stress or trauma on the embryo, infant or child which could either allow in more toxins (oxidative stress, pitocin, epidural, aluminum and other junk from vaccines) or create a state of urgency in which the astrocytes are not as available to communicate the development of a strong blood-brain barrier (Alvarez, J., Katayama, T. and Pratt, A., 2013), thereby possibly compromising long-term health (see section on long-term health and the blood-brain barrier). Further if the pineal gland is experiencing metal toxicity from vaccines or is calcified from poor nutrition and fluoride or is being bathed in radiation from cell phones, well frankly, I hypothesize that things like circadian rhythms and endothelial cells aren't going to work right "at best" and "at worst" result in a major health issue. **The pineal gland influences genetic codes that determine the constitution of blood-brain barrier cells. If you mess with the pineal gland you might not get strong blood-brain barrier cells along with other major functions compromised.** Don't worry … the book gets lighter from here. My hope is that this information comes to make sense as we move through the book, supporting scientifically why you might make certain decisions. Don't forget to come back here for certain sections … please.

*****One of my clients said she is now having to undue, some of the standard care procedures that she believes caused autism and mutism in her daughter. This client would not want you to go through, what she's been through.**

*****I want to make clear that I believe most organizations and doctors in implementing standard care procedures want the highest and best good for children, mothers, fathers and families. I think that we are all learning and integrating as we go along. In sharing what I have experienced personally and through research, I also want the highest and best good for children, mothers, fathers and families. I vision that we all work together!

3. CONCEPTION and PREGNANCY:

Heal first, baby second: I am going to strongly recommend, that before anyone makes a baby!!! that they get thoroughly looked over by a skilled local modern day **1. Energy Worker/Shaman** (there are lots of them) and **2. Acupuncturist** and **3. Emotion Code Therapist** (who can heal stuck emotions and ancestral line issues) while ingesting homeopathic doses of **4. Ayahuasca** (plant medicine that moves out old memories and trauma, available through Celletech … http://celletech.com). I know that I sound like I'm kidding, I'm not. It may be the most important thing I say to you. Psychotherapy is great, but you may not have two to ten years to get through all your layers of trauma and family history, past lives and so on. The above mentioned therapies should be sincerely researched as a fast track to pulling the junk off of you and getting to your best mama-self or best papa-self. It is no one's fault exactly, life is a beautiful jungle. Anyway, if you don't do the work ahead of time, you may be launched into your own unhealed traumas and early childhood history pretty much as soon as your little one gets out of the gate (please see final section on healing emotions). Trust me on this one … children push you to evolve whatever you didn't evolve on your own. Newborn phase over, Baby daddy and I suddenly began looking at each other from our unhealed stuff and possibly two or three past lives, resulting in years of nails and claws … retraction only recent. Further, I have played out painful things with my daughter that could have been avoided.

Love covenant all night long: OK, now that you have been all shined up by your local medicine woman, it's time for conception! That's right … how do we make the baby? We begin with particle exchanging (sometimes all night long). So, whenever you are about to have sex, make love, do the wild thing, please put a covenant of love around the process. It could be an intention, a prayer, or an invocation to your favorite angel, saint or goddess. A law of love in sex makes more particles of love on the planet or in baby-making, more particles of love in baby. You could be married for ten years, or on date number five with your match.com fellow, just about to make "the big move," or one bar stool away from your one night stand. Love covenant the heck out of them! I recommend a condom for the latter two scenarios and a future plan for baby-making (which includes the abovementioned healing work). Though seriously no judgment, babies are made past midnight between men and women who don't know much about each other, doesn't mean we can't have love covenants (and then do the abovementioned personal healing work while pregnant).

While this may seem to be a spiritual idea or some "out there" new age concept, a love covenant is actually a direction to the glial cells to send messages to the hypothalamus to produce super love hormones such as oxytocin. Therefore when conception occurs oxytocin supports a stronger biological environment for the sperm and egg meeting (if you know what I mean). In addition, the glial cells directing love partner to partner, means more oxytocin for the benefit of everyone involved (if you know what I mean).

Radial glial cells form close to conception: There are all different kinds of glial cells, with all different kinds of functions. Radial glial cells form in your baby close to the time of conception, and many radial glia, spring into astrocytes at birth (Koob, 2009). Now, the fact that these radial glial cells explode into astrocytes at birth (remember astrocytes are your motherboard), makes me believe that we have found the biological component to our souls. So let's begin talking love to our baby's glial cells from the point of conception and beyond. It could be the very thing that makes for a calm, peaceful, intelligent, and happy infant, then child, then adult. **Note:** When babies are forming and into their first year of life, there is a great opportunity to allow brain connections that strengthen love, balance and emotional well-being. By their spirit (radial glial to astrocytes), they have beautifully **already** written brains and they rely on you to preserve that for them, until they can manage their own environments. We can truly make a new generation of people by telling our growing babies how kind and wonderful they are. Please make them of your love (which will allow them to be their spirit in their body) not a history of challenge, if you can help it. Personally, I have deeply loved my daughter and … I am sure she will spend weeks with a Shaman in Peru sometime in her mid-twenties, where she entangles from all of her mother issues. Sorry honey, I love you!

Here's how I think positive thought and love, are passed on to the embryo: Your astrocytes and glial cells send messages via calcium waves into the womb, to the radial glia of your growing baby. *The more a thought is repeated, the more calcium waves flow, from your glia (and theoretically to baby glia), fostering positive connections in neuronal network activity* (Hines and Haydon, 2014). When you beat on a drum, more sound waves are produced. When you say more words of love, more waves of love are produced in the brain and body. You are literally creating the molecular structure of the radial glia and when they spring into astrocytes at birth, it's all good news. Unhealthy genes are more likely to be expressed in unhealthy, stressed environments (Gosselin et al., 2010). Good genes are more likely to be expressed in healthy environments (Gosselin et al., 2010). You are creating a serene loving place … better genes are chosen. (If you are an American, your life is likely to be at best very busy, and at worst, coupled with life circumstances that are super challenging. Most of us live imperfect lives … uh, if you could see me, my hand is raised on this. Do the best you can, and say, "I love you," a lot.)

Difficulty conceiving: I am so sorry if this is so (difficulty conceiving). Since we're getting so close, I might as well tell you, I have actually been divorced twice. I married when I was 26 to a very kind person. We had a log cabin in the woods, an outback station wagon and were making at least a weekly attempt at conceiving a child. But, I had all kinds of late blooming irregular period stuff. We worked with a fertility doctor and I even took fertility drugs (before my no drug, totally holistic lifestyle kicked in). None of the fertility stuff worked and the free spirit in me (at age 29) left that life (free spirit is arguably a fear of commitment). Don't worry the first X is really happy now with kids and everything! I am so happy for him. Anyway, when I got together with the baby daddy (five years later and a musician in between) I thought I couldn't have children. Baby Daddy moved up to Vermont (where I was living at the time). I owned a tiny holistic, health and beauty shop, called The Practical Universe, where I learned all kinds of things on health and nutrition, but especially about essential oils (which are important in their own right, but also in coming sections). Superfoods are another thing I learned about while in VT. I began taking maca root powder, a plant known to boost energy, libido and support hormonal balance. All of sudden, my periods were regular and a year or so later, in a not so planned way, at age 36, my daughter was conceived in true and deep love. Please research maca root and other holistic natural fertility treatments, such as hypnosis, acupuncture, nutrition and chiropractic. **Note:** While conception was not exactly planned, Baby Daddy and I had several conversations to the effect of … "there is definitely a spirit knocking at our door." I believe that the maca root helped get my daughter through and … was likely her suggestion.

Conception, emotion and Candace Pert: Candace Pert, totally awesome biologist (now deceased, bless her), taught us that the hypothalamus produces peptide hormones specific to, specific emotions, i.e. fear peptide or happy peptide (Pert, C., 1999). Peptides act as keys in cell to cell communication and when the peptide chains are based on negative emotion from old memories, I imagine there are problems. When you heal memories and stuck emotions, theoretically you break down those unwanted peptide chains. Please heal in whatever way you can. It will help, not just in difficulty conceiving, but in everything.

OK conception accomplished hopefully with great love and some rockin' good times! Here's a few extra TIPS to support your growing baby right down to its molecules:

Listen to your instincts: Instincts (I think) are the most clear when you're pregnant. At conception, you have engaged the care of a living organism, who has a path for life. If you listen, you will find that what works so beautifully for whales or dolphins, or birds, or any form of nature, will work for you and for the being you are co-creating.

Beautiful Music: We've all heard it … play your baby music that's fun, soothing or meditative. Brain waves and beautiful music make a harmonious baby, so it's worth saying again and again. Here's what I think is happening … those radial glia are recording the vibration of all that beautiful music stimulating well-being that lasts a lifetime. Baby Daddy played the didgeridoo into my pregnant belly and would play it often for my daughter as an infant and toddler. High frequency energy busts out low frequency energy, like how the sun's rays lift water into the air. The didgeridoo measures at a high frequency and so does your singing! High frequency is associated with a strong life force. **Note:** I have a friend couple who are both musicians and own a music shop. Through pregnancy and infancy, their two boys were exposed to bands, music lessons, jams, etc. and their boys have met developmental milestones very, very early. I am willing to bet that it has everything to do with the music.

Search Item: Music and Brain Development.

Speak only kind words as much as possible: When you are angry with your partner, write them a letter. Don't let harsh arguments be present in your pregnancy. If it happens, clear the exchange by saying to your baby, ***"I am so sorry. Please forgive me. I love you and thank you."*** During pregnancy, I was cognizant of the effects of negative emotion on my growing baby. However, my life circumstances had stress, anxiety, anger and loss in them (insert baby daddy) that I did not always clear or heal before it threw up out of my mouth. **Note:** I do not blame the baby daddy for the pieces I am responsible for, and I am responsible for loads of parent error. (Don't worry about me though I can recognize my faults while still loving myself as a mother and person.) Anyway, that "throw up" out my mouth, to some degree, became negative thought and emotion, passed to my originally perfect daughter. OK, "originally perfect daughter" might be a little dramatic, with a twinge of residual mother guilt.

On with it! As my daughter was developing her personality between age two and three, I could see that she carried the intensity of her parents' struggle. The quality of that behavior in her was relative to what she had absorbed, and I didn't want it to be a part of the personality that she developed. It really wasn't her true nature, it was absorbed emotion. In order to help heal this, I connected with alternative practitioners who work with emotions and energy in the body (Emotion Code Therapist), to release these issues and dissolve these patterns within her. You don't have to let it get that far. If you can really find ways to divert your negative emotion when you're pregnant (and through their development), you will theoretically have a more congenial child. Believe that their growing cells are intelligent, and record, and remember. What pattern do you want them to live by?

Search Item: *Zero Limits*, by Joe Vitale ... This book offers the rationale behind saying ***"I am sorry, please forgive me, I love you and thank you"*** a sort of molecular restart button.

More reasons to say "I love you and thank you" all the time: A scientist named Masaru Emoto conducted a number of studies on the effects of intention on water. Water that had the words "I love you and thank you" intended upon it formed the most elaborate, and beautiful crystals. Words like, "stupid" and "you fool" made cloudy, half-formed, ugly crystals (Emoto, 2004). We are made of more than 70% water, we might as well go for the "I love and thank you" water in our babies and children. I will again venture to say that you'll be making a striking effect on those very important glial cells.

Search Item: Dr. Masaru Emoto and all of his books ... *The Hidden Messages in Water, The Secret of Water, The Healing Power of Water* and more!

Heart Song: In some Native American cultures a heart song was created for babies during pregnancy or at birth. The song was sung when the baby felt upset or was sick to restore comfort and well-being. You can do this as well ... anything small and sweet will do, something about the essence you feel for your baby. It could be their name, or one word, or an entire song. Don't worry about performing on stage, it's just for your baby. Even if you feel you cannot sing well, sing often ... your voice creates a bonding rhythm. **Note:** You can create a heart song for your child even if they're ten years old. The heart connection between a parent and their child can be strengthened at any age. Well, I am not so sure a heart song would go over great with your teenager. You will likely embarrass everyone, so skip it, if they've hit puberty (or just sing it quietly to yourself ... they will feel the love and then probably clean their room and do their homework without you asking).

Eat Organic please: Eat lots of organic greens, nuts/beans, citrus fruits, and organic almond, coconut or hemp milk. Drink a daily, natural protein shake ... it may be the very thing that keeps you feeling great throughout your pregnancy. In the very beginning of my second trimester, I nearly passed out at Home Depot. Turns out this green leaf chomping vegetarian (me), needed double the protein, iron and nutrients, and so the daily protein powder/organic spinach shake (as recommended by a friend) that I added to my life, did the trick. I know it sounds gross, but maple syrup and organic fruit disguise the spinach. Anyway, please eat simply in organic beauty and supplement the heck out of yourself, preferably through herbs (like Rosehips tea) and superfoods (that you have researched as safe for pregnant women ... David Wolfe is your guru on this). If you nutritionally match what you require, it is less likely, that you will have unhealthy cravings. Good living organic food and superfoods are really one of the most effective ways to turn on healthy genetics, and to keep the not so nice genetics, like your Aunt Mary's long nose hairs and grumpy temperament, in the off position.

Search Item: Superfoods for pregnant women

Natural body care: Through pregnancy and breastfeeding, please use natural toothpaste, deodorant, nail polish, make-up, hair dye, soaps/shampoos, bug repellant, sunscreen and tampons/pads … all available at Whole Foods. All of that toxic crap typically put in these products should **never** be put in the body, but please especially keep your developing embryo, newborn and infant from being exposed to that toxic crap. Thank you, you are awesome! If you are worried about prices at Whole Foods, consider that the extra money that you spend means so much to the earth because of what and how the product was made. And … employees at Whole Foods earn a livable wage, get a discount on their food and (I think) are treated with great respect (I am sure there a few A-hole bosses here and there). Whole Foods also donates some of their profit to great causes! This is how the world changes because everybody benefits in a "sustain our mother (earth)" sort-of-way! Other big chain grocery stores are becoming more and more earth supportive … let's keep going and thank you!

Epigenetics: Check out **http://pregnancy.thesfile.com/epigenetics/** which gives information about influencing and changing genetics. It indicates that pregnancy is a very important point in silencing genes you don't want and encouraging the expression of the ones you do. _**(If there was only one search item that you had the energy to investigate, please make it this one!)**_

4. ULTRASOUNDS:

*****Ultrasounds should only be used when <u>absolutely</u> medically necessary.

SPECIAL NOTE: Please imagine how the high decibel sound waves and the high heat of an ultrasound might be affecting the very important systems of your developing embryo and how their radial glia (that will later become astrocytes) might be feeling. I am theorizing that the radial glia register the sound and heat as something pretty urgent and therefore do not communicate homeostasis ("I love you wind and wild flower harmony"), they communicate from activation ("Oh my gosh, what they hell is going on? It's so hot and loud!!!"). The central nervous system changes when glial cells are activated (Alvarez, J., Katayama, T. and Prat, A., 2013).

Ultrasounds can cause problems: Check out **www.alternamoms.com/ultrasound** which hosts a series of peer reviewed research articles linking ultrasounds to low birth weight in babies, changes in the babies' cell growth, speech delays and learning problems. If there are physical concerns during pregnancy, mothers and fathers should absolutely consider an ultrasound, because it is the best way to find out what the problem is. However, the choice to get an ultrasound should be done with thorough research about why it's being conducted. The provider and parents must weigh the decision, choosing between a problem an ultrasound could reveal, verses a problem it could cause. Remember **Gut + Research = Highest and Best Decision.**

*****Please Google **Ultrasounds Cause Autism** and see what you can find! There is information out there to this regard. If ultrasounds can cause Autism in one child, it could potentially cause different problems in another child, depending upon genetic history. I theorize that if the embryo is stressed by the ultrasound process, then bad history genetics could express in the radial glia.

Ultrasound registers at 100 decibels: In an article published in PubMed, titled *Obstrecical Ultrasound: Can the fetus hear the wave and feel the heat?* (2012), researchers placed a tiny hydrophone in the uterus while the woman was having an ultrasound. When the ultrasound probe was turned toward the hydrophone, it registered at 100 decibels, "as loud as a subway train coming into the station" (Abramowicz, JS, Kemkau, FW & Merz, E., 2012). I know that ultrasounds have provided important information and have saved the lives of mothers and babies (which clearly falls under medically indicated), but "medically indicated" is the key. You, as the mother or father, must be strong in this, because in the medical community, ultrasounds have become a routine recommendation. Get a second opinion. Again, please use **Gut + Research = Highest and Best Decision.** Ask a midwife for the information you might get from an ultrasound. Some of it, she or he, can tell you without looking.

Check out the article *Routine Ultrasound Testing Not Proven Safe for Pregnant Women* retrieved from www.naturalnews.com/ultrasoundpregantwomentesting which indicates that in the 1970s ultrasounds were thought to be safe because of the very low scanning intensities. In 1993, high output machines were allowed to scan babies at eight times the tolerable level without conducting any epidemiological studies." Bones and surrounding tissues are heated by each scan, up to six degrees higher than the maximum determined level of safety. "This can lead to a **disruption in cell function and permeability**, bleeding, and can have adverse effects on early fetal development" (Heimer, M., ND, 2013). A further part of article states:

Ultrasound studies done on animals have shown **cell abnormalities**, to several generations, brain hemorrhages, lung damage, slow loco-motor and learning abilities that worsened with longer exposure, and neuronal migration abnormalities consistent with autism and dyslexia in humans. Mice exposed to 600 minutes of ultrasound survived, no longer than ten days (Heimer, M., ND, 2013).

I am not sure of current output levels of ultrasounds. I heard from one of my clients that there are newer higher depth ultrasounds, which frankly scares me for babies. I know if you currently Google FDA and ultrasounds, a whole lot pops up saying "FDA recommends against" or warns against ultrasounds other than medical necessity. Stuff like heating tissues and cavitations (small bubbles) in tissues is part of their warning. (When people have strokes or traumatic brain injury there is cavitations in the brain, imagine baby lungs or other organs.) I believe there should be a standing law … *No ultrasounds unless truly documented as medically necessary for specific conditions with physician accountability and possibly one ultrasound for women over the age of thirty-five.* **Doctors are typically kind, upstanding people and if given a limit with supportive reasoning, this could be an easy change.**

Don't let someone convince you to no longer trust yourself: At each trimester, there are different expectations that your provider will want to standardize in your pregnancy. My instinct told me to do virtually none of the typical, most especially, my law of "no ultrasound!" (I was over age thirty-five by one year. If you are healthy, you may not need one.) When I was influenced by fear at times, I had a stronger overriding feeling, "It's a girl and everything is going to be fine." My baby girl was eighteen days beyond what was thought to be her due date (I believe her due date was the day she came), no ultrasound and everything went beautifully. At one point in my pregnancy, I spoke with a provider who told me a scary story about a pregnant woman who could have benefited from an ultrasound. I really had to search and secure the strong feeling I had, that basically said, "NO ULTRASOUND." I'm not saying that your gut won't tell you that you need one, because maybe it will, but please investigate what you really, really feel (and thoroughly research), not what someone else scares you into feeling. Trust yourself.

Search Item: Effects of ultrasounds on the brain of the fetus.

Instinct for no ultrasound: When I was about ten days past what was estimated to be my due date, my midwife recommended an ultrasound to check on the baby's condition. My midwife was and is beyond amazing, as a person and provider, and my instinct/researched decision to have no ultrasound challenged her. Yet, she still stood by me, allowing me to trust myself. I am forever, grateful for that.

*****If a recommendation for an ultrasound is made, ask your doctor what indications, deem it medically necessary.

*****I don't want to be the kid with the BB gun shooting balloons down at the "reveal the sex of the baby" party, but **<u>finding out the sex of your baby is not medically necessary.</u>** The FDA advises against this now common practice.

*****Some families are getting multiple ultrasounds through the course of their pregnancy. This is very much against all governing bodies for best baby health. It's like a Swedish family going to the equator for a beach day without sunscreen saying "we will be fine." (Please always use natural sunscreen.)

*****Consider asking your doctor to check your babies' heartbeat with a stethoscope, rather than a Doppler.

5. HOME BIRTH/NATURAL BIRTH:

Home births/Midwives: I am a super big fan of home births and I believe whenever possible we should be birthing our babies at home. Birthing a baby in a warm, loving, low stimulus environment like your own home, is how a being imprints calm in their central nervous system (of lifelong importance). Maybe you have a chaotic, emotionally charged household, with a bunch of squatting relatives, and a drum kit, but don't completely rule out the home birth just yet. You could kick out the relatives, put on some Bach or Reggae, light a few candles, and call a midwife. Anything is possible! In any case, I believe babies need to be born into peaceful and calm environments, which theoretically creates peaceful and calm babies who grow up into lovely, healthy, serene or appropriately exuberant people.

Home births allow you to choose how long you labor, how you labor and how you position yourself for birth. Most importantly, home births allow you to connect to the natural birthing instincts present in mammals and present in you. Please, always work with a trusted midwife when choosing a home birth. **Note:** As a psychotherapist, I work with people who have problems on the other end of life. If people have a traumatic birth, bonding issues, physical separation from mother or caregiver, it could result in adult anxiety, depression and possibly physical ailments. I believe the formula of **Calm birth + Closeness with Caregiver = Strength/Well-being of Adult.**

The trend toward home births is rising and midwives are very skilled and knowledgeable about every stage of pregnancy and birth. In my experience, midwives offer the standard care information along with an entire toolbox of holistic options. At each trimester, my midwife offered me the option of choosing procedures typically offered by an OBGYN which I mostly, declined. She also suggested foods, herbs, remedies and homeopathy, which eased the course of pregnancy and labor. Love her!

At the time of my daughter's birth, I was living in an artist cooperative, a lovely three bedroom apartment in New Britain, CT. Neighborhood not so great, but I had a good view of the sky, and found it was typically better not to look down at what was transpiring in the parking lot (just a little prostitution, a few drug deals, it's all good). My home birth included two friends (excellent massage, back rubbing friends), two midwives and one baby daddy. Plus, we were blessed with a whole slew of family and friend prayers keeping us well. Talking. Singing. Drumming. A little birth pooling it. A couple of moments of …. "I can't go on any more." Then some "I WILL do it" and some pushing on the bed, some screaming, some nearly breaking the baby daddy's arm, and out comes my new baby boy. "What? I thought I was having a girl." In my delirium and an umbilical cord crossing over the privates, I thought my beautiful baby girl was a boy, and then she peed on me, and went right to nursing …and yes … **a rush of incredible love**. Next, tear off birth sheets. Clean sheets ready beneath. I am in my own bed, eating my own food, feeling the comfort that was built during pregnancy (despite city happenings). I am grateful for my birth team, for all those family/friend prayers (you know who you are) and for the serenity of the artist cooperative apartment that I called home at that time (I kind of move around a lot). **Note:** Birthing my daughter was a deeply spiritual and physical experience for me. I am purposely making it sound so matter-of-fact so you'll feel like you could easily have a home birth. Is it working? But seriously … You are a woman (unless you are actually a man reading this book, then please say this to your woman). I will begin again … You are a woman with a divine force in you so vast and so unstoppable that you literally have universe-birthing-a-star power at the moment when your baby is arriving!!! Stop looking at the white coat for the answers, rip off the hospital monitors and claim that force! It is yours and if you want your child to have it … show them what you got!

Ok, back to the matter-of-fact …

Then the birth team went home and it's just another day, except there's now a super new awesome human added to the world. You really don't need a whole bunch of fuss over something the body can naturally do, just saying. Imagine if we were brought to the hospital when we were making the baby, hooked up to monitors and a bunch of people hovering around your "process." I think much fewer babies would be made, natural sex drive, um, lost in that environment. Natural birth drives aught not be so controlled either. There were things for me about birthing that were mind challenging at times, but so is a marathon and people just do it. Actually, birth can be far easier than a marathon. The idea that women can "just do it," (sorry I didn't mean to get all Nike on you) has been whittled away. Don't get me wrong, I know things are evolving, I mean in the forties and fifties woman were knocked out with the twilight drug and then woke up to a new baby. I guess, I think we need to honor how special birth is while getting a little stronger and more confident about the body's abilities … "I know how to go the bathroom, I know how to have sex and I know how to have a baby." Then we won't be so damned stressed about the process because stress makes more pain, and fear makes birth seem like a coming trauma. It's not (see hypnobirthing section in coming pages)! We are not lab rats (sorry to the rats) or intensive care patients (sorry about this also), we are WOMEN! You need a bed, a midwife, maybe one or two supportive friends or family members, a baby daddy is great (but not totally necessary, could be a sperm donor and a lesbian lover, right?) a couple sets of sheets, maybe a cry out to whatever God you believe in and your breath. Please, please don't make it into something traumatic (like it has become in certain, uh, hospitals), because then the rhythm of birth is lost and so is the strength and authority of what's inside you … and that is the extraordinary part, which brings creation into form and is almost beyond comprehension. It is you and your baby, you got this!

I will sincerely never forget that first night with my beautiful little being, her life force, so sweet and so strong, and "Oh my gosh, this is my baby." I really did say things like, "she's perfect" and "just how I imagined her to be." I am very blessed.

*****I know that most women can birth at home naturally, and I know that there are situations in a small percentage of women who require higher levels of support. If you are so very blessed to be a healthy woman, than I encourage you to consider a home/natural birth. If you do require higher levels of support, you can still access that divine birth-a-star force in you. Whatever your circumstance, call it in … pretty please!

Natural induction methods: I was eighteen days beyond when we expected my daughter to come. It felt to me that she needed to gestate perhaps, a little longer. Being fixed on due dates can cause premature induction which can mean that systems (like the central nervous system) in the baby's body have not been properly developed. ***Induction should <u>NEVER</u> occur because of lack of patience or someone's schedule. A strengthened, properly developed central nervous system could mean a lifelong difference mentally, physically and emotionally for your child.*** My daughter has a strong constitution, has rarely been ill and certainly knows who she is. Those eighteen days meant something to this regard … and no one can tell me different.

However, with all that said … I did recognize that there was another issue which felt like an emotional block in me the size of Gibraltar. I tried a few herbal induction methods (please consult with a naturopath/midwife), with not too much success (for my issues!) though it could be for you and has been for many other women. As I was nearing day eighteen past the anticipated due date, I then went to an acupuncturist as recommended by my midwife. A few needles here and a few needles there and I launched into labor before I got out the door. By the way, acupuncture is generally not painful and it was not for me. This method certainly unblocked whatever blocks needed to be unblocked, in order to get things flowing. It should be noted that acupuncture does not create a rapid unnatural induction, like another drug we all know (wink, wink begins with a P).

Long labors are normal: Having a long labor is often associated with challenge. However, the natural progression of contractions that move slowly can be part of a very healthy birth. Speediness in labor is a cultural mindset and I had to shift how I thought. The length of my labor, thirty hours total, and fifteen hours of active labor (when contractions are five minutes apart), allowed for a natural opening of my vagina and a calm transition for my daughter from the womb to the world. I believe if birth is unnaturally speedy, it can create a condition of shock for the newborn, where they begin their life with a trauma.

Please look into HYPNOBIRTHING: Training the mind to feel calm and reduce fears, as with hypnobirthing, could be an essential tool in keeping your glial cells from moving into an activated state. If the astrocytes do not send a message about a coming trauma (as many women think/feel about birth), these important communicators can theoretically maintain balance of neurotransmitters and the pain networks will not be sent messages to react. Women using hypnobirthing are among the most confident about birth that I have come across, possibly because they do not think of birth as a coming trauma.

I didn't take any hypnobirthing classes while pregnant (dang!) and I did experience some pain in labor. However, I did use visualization, which made a direct physical change. Prior to giving birth, I had read of a woman who repeatedly visualized her vagina, changing and opening wide enough, for her baby to travel easily through. It really worked for me. The midwives were surprised that I had not a single tare with a nearly ten pound baby. The mind does control your physical experience! **Side note:** Also to this mind/body regard … I said repeatedly in the laboring process to my daughter, "My heart beats with your heart beat." The midwives regularly checked our hearts and found that our beats were exactly the same. Using a stethoscope, the midwives checked and double checked … because they said they had never come across, <u>exact</u> mother/baby heartbeats.

Search Items: There are women through hypnobirthing, who have reported orgasmic-like labor and delivery of their babies. I recently met a woman who had exactly that experience. She said of the contractions, "I didn't want it to stop" and something about "amazing" and "blissful." So, yes, definitely search hypnobirthing classes in your area. Check out the book *Birth Without Fear* and the Bradley Method, similar to hypnobirthing (Thanks Ms. Gibson for these recommendations).

*****Remember that women have been birthing babies since the beginning of time, in the woods, in huts, igloos and homes. Giving birth is not an illness! Please do it naturally, you really can! I mean it!* **Natural birth vs. unnatural birth:** Please consider a natural birth. Having a baby who enters the world clearly, without the haze of drugs, allows for the highest level of the natural love chemical, oxytocin to be released. This love chemical shared between the baby and mother forges the greatest bond at the most important moment. The bond between the mother and baby is not "just a nice concept." Think about those brain cells, the astrocytes that explode at birth, literally, our intelligence. A natural birth means they're flooded with all those love chemicals that make the beginning of how one thinks and behaves. Now think how the radial glial explode into astrocytes at birth. Now think about astrocytes exploding into a dulled by drugs environment, or possibly, exploding less, because of that dulled by drugs environment.

6. HOSPITAL BIRTH:

Before we go on, think about how weird this question sounds ... In what percentage of mammals is an unnatural birth necessary? My guess ... just higher than none. Why can't the (supposedly) most evolved species on the planet have close to that number ... just higher than none? Well, system programmed fear is a good answer and money another good answer. I love you, let's go on.

Side note: Natural births occur in hospitals and birthing centers! This is awesome and is becoming more and more common and supported! Let's keep going!!!

I believe that epidurals confuse the natural birth instincts possibly causing the side effects detailed below: The National Institute of Health made available the article titled, *Unintended effects of epidural analgesia during labor: a systematic review.* It indicated that "there is sufficient evidence to conclude that epidurals are associated with a lower rate of spontaneous vaginal delivery, a higher rate of instrumental vaginal delivery and longer labors." The article also stated that "further research about unintended effects of epidurals is necessary, so that women can truly make an informed decision," Lieberman, E., O'Donoghue, C. (2002). Check out The American Pregnancy Associations' list of Epidural side effects:

> Though research is somewhat ambiguous, most studies suggest that some babies will have trouble "latching on" causing breastfeeding difficulties. Other studies suggest that a baby might experience respiratory depression, fetal malpositioning, and an increase in fetal heart rate variability, thus increasing the need for forceps, vacuum, cesarean deliveries and episiotomies (americanpregnancy.org/labornbirth/epidural).

Epidurals and pitocin can go hand and hand. The epidural slows the contractions then the pitocin is recommended to speed up the labor. In May of 2012, Evidence Based Birth published an online article titled, *What is the Evidence for pitocin Augmentation?* (evidencebasedbirth.com). This article indicates that while pitocin is a synthetic form of oxytocin, it does not produce more love, it increases the force, frequency and duration of uterine contractions. The FDA marks pitocin with a black box warning, which is their strongest warning for drugs and says "induction should only be used when medically necessary" (evidencebasedbirth.com). **I think we need to listen to the FDA a little more, both with ultrasounds and pitocin use. I mean aren't we supposed to? FDA warnings are not "just a suggestion" right?** The article begins by asking the question of women, who have gone to the hospital <u>already</u> in spontaneous labor, if they have then heard "Let's start the pitocin." Standardizing pitocin use has set into our culture and we must unset it. The article states that the list of potential side effects are long (please research) which include heart problems and uterine rupture for mothers, and heart problems and permanent brain damage for baby. The article further indicated that pitocin is meant to reduce C-sections and has not, and a doctor's indication for "augmentation" of pitocin is primarily to speed up slow labor.

If pitocin is recommended, the article suggests that you respond to your provider by saying "Am I OK.? Is my baby OK? Let's wait a little longer." Another reason to research a home birth ....no one is going to ask you about pitocin in the heat of labor. You're going to let nature take its course and trust it. Believe me I do understand why you'd want to make things less painful and speed things up. As said above, I had over thirty hours of total labor, and more than fifteen hours of active labor. However, labor is long sometimes, because it's naturally meant to create a peaceful entrance for your newborn into the world. I believe rushing the birth through pitocin can create shock and trauma in the baby. The difference is like saying, "Breathe, take your time, all is well," verses "Hurry up, go, get out, something's wrong." No one would dream of giving pitocin to a whale or a dolphin or other mammal, it'd be considered unethical. Nature births young at its own pace. Humans are the only species that can't wait.

Search Item: Check out the difference between oxytocin (waves of deep nurturing love) and pitocin (rapid waves of get out of my body as fast as you can) … http://pregnancy.about.com/od/induction/a/pitocindiffers.htm. I think there must be a big difference, which is why nature doesn't use pitocin. Please refer to the section 2 information on the pineal gland, blood-brain barrier and glial cells, considering how all that pitocin emergency rapid firing, could impact very important brain functions.

Hospital Birth Procedures: While I have a strong leaning toward home birthing, midwives and natural births, many of my dearest friends, coworkers and family members have had beautiful, healthy babies in hospitals. I want to honor that as important because I love them, their decisions and their wonderful children. So I hope that if you have decided to hospital birth your child, you will consider this next section and integrate it, into your decision-making, with honor from me, in whatever you choose.

I interviewed Newborn Specialist Lindsay Gibson (www.ready-baby.com) to gain an inside view of hospital birthing, since I didn't have one. Ms. Gibson has an eight year-old daughter, and at the time of interview was seven months pregnant. She primarily works with mothers post birth, but she also provides education for pregnant women. Ms. Gibson reported that a main concern about birthing in a hospital is the pressure to labor faster which she said is truly destructive to a woman who would normally follow the rhythm of her baby and body.

Ms. Gibson stated that although she did not have a C-section with her first child, one in three women now have them. She also reported that some hospitals have a large digital clock timer visible to women while laboring, and if ten hours pass (or other identified time frame) and no baby, women are whisked away for a C-section. (If a woman was pressured in this way to have an orgasm, she wouldn't have one. The vagina just does not work that way. I said that, not Ms. Gibson.) Ms Gibson indicated that these sorts of psychological pressures make it incredibly difficult to birth naturally and for labor to run its course as it should. Please research how many hours of labor your hospital allows.

Side note on "one in three women has a C-section": I spoke with a woman who intended to have her baby in a birthing center. When she arrived, one centimeter dilated, she was sent away because they could not keep her until she was three centimeters dilated. She did not want to go home and so asked her husband to take her to the emergency room at a different hospital. After laboring at the new hospital for 20 hours, she was told that she had four hours left before all of her attendants would be going home. The doctors then recommended a C-section, since she had not labored fast enough. Due to the enormous pressures of that system, she agreed. This is why one in three women has a C-section.

It is important to note that birthing centers give you up to forty-eight hours to labor, hospitals sometimes twenty-four or less, and home births, for the most part, have no time to consider.

Contractions, monitors and fear of pain: Ms. Gibson indicated that mothers are strapped to monitors for nurses to check contractions and heart rates, which keep women from laboring in different positions or walking around. The monitors' indication of coming contractions fuels the fear of pain. Rather than allowing a woman to connect with her breath and possibly peaceful visualizations, there are loud beeps and noises that disturb her well-being. Ms. Gibson also said that women are frequently checked to measure dilation when this is an unnecessary practice and again pressures the mother to move along disturbing her natural rhythm. Ms. Gibson recommends that in a healthy pregnancy and birthing situation (as most are), dilation could be checked when you first arrive and not again until you feel the baby coming ... which a mother instinctively knows.

Side note on exhausted hospital staff and doctors: I have a ton of compassion for doctors and hospital staff who are exhausted and want to go home to their lives and families. **This is why the system is not matched to natural labor and birth, because the system should not be exhausting the provider to the point that they are looking to speed things up.** Ms. Gibson stated that, in many European countries, births are only attended by a physician if there is a serious complication. Otherwise, it's midwives who are the primary caregivers in typical births. Please research.

Interview Your OBGYN: Ms. Gibson encourages women, to feel strong and to advocate for their natural birthing process. She recommends an interview with one's OBGYN prior to selection, asking questions such as:
1.) Will you adhere to a birth plan if there are no complications? (The birth plan is your written decisions about how you want to labor and birth your child.)
2.) How do you feel about prolonged labor?
3.) When would you conduct a C-section and why?
4.) Can I birth my baby in any position I want?
5.) When would you conduct an episiotomy (please research) and do I have the right to refuse this procedure?
6.) For what reasons would you separate me from my baby? (Love you doctor/nurse, but I will take you out if you try to.)
7.) How do you feel about delayed cord clamping (see the section on Placenta/Cord Cutting)?

Ms. Gibson said that a woman has the right to refuse any procedure issued and that a clear understanding of what is necessary and unnecessary in a healthy birth, brings confidence to the family in making their decisions. Remember **Gut + Research = Highest and Best Decision.**

Hospital post birth procedures: Another important piece of information given by Ms. Gibson involves the standard hospital bath post birth. First and foremost, the baby should not be separated from the mother unless there is a serious complication. Secondly, Ms. Gibson indicated that a baby is generally born with remnants of vernix, a byproduct of the placenta, remaining on its skin. The vernix is an antioxidant, a skin cleanser, a moisturizer, a temperature regulator, and is antimicrobial. Let it dissolve and absorb into the skin. Ms. Gibson also said that the bath exposes the baby to chemicals found in standard soaps and shampoos. Babies come from the most sterile environment, the mother's womb, and do not need to be bathed for six weeks (other than a warm washcloth to their bottoms), said Ms. Gibson. She added that, if a parent absolutely wants a bath immediately, she respects the decision, but recommends that they bring their own natural soap such as California Baby, Honest Company, or another organic soap.

Ms. Gibson recommends that families research all of the possibly unnecessary procedures that occur within a hospital birth, such as the antibiotic ointment, rubbed over babies' eyes at birth. The antibiotic is supposed to be applied in cases where the mother has a sexually transmitted disease. This procedure has become standard and is very uncomfortable for the baby and! ... I theorize that giving unnecessary antibiotics could confuse the immune function because the body could believe there is a toxin to fight. Now your baby is not spending all of its energy on critical development, the body is possibly confused and must focus its attention on the messages related to the antibiotic. Please also consider that your little one feels pain, and even the smallest of discomforts means something to their underdeveloped central nervous system. Please research all hospital procedures and think carefully about unnecessary ones.

Circumcision is an unnecessary trauma: One of these (torturous) unnecessary and painful hospital procedures is circumcision. Please be clear that circumcision does not create more cleanliness, as was once thought (please research). In fact, generations of men have begun their life with a serious, serious trauma to their sexual organ for a misguided reason. This could explain the dysfunction and disconnection from emotion and sexuality in some men. Ms. Gibson states that these little human beings are enduring a procedure that no grown man would choose to endure.

Ms. Gibson also stated that, in circumcision, the infant is taken from the mother, strapped down, and essentially traumatized. She adds that if you absolutely feel that you want this procedure conducted, be present with your baby for closeness, and to ensure that the utmost gentleness is used. (Although, the mother will then also be traumatized from watching her baby experience this painful process). Fortunately, word has spread about declining this procedure, and Ms. Gibson said that at least 50% of the population is now uncircumcised. Please join them. This could mean a world of difference is raising peaceful, loving boys into men.

*****The American Academy of Pediatrics has stated that "in no uncertain terms," "there is no, absolute, medical indication, for routine circumcision, of the newborn" www.medicinenet.com/circumcision.

*****When you are deciding about circumcision, please remember that cortisol released in the brain, from stress and trauma, can turn on unhealthy gene codes (Gosselin et al., 2010).

Skin to skin with newborn: Ms. Gibson adds that the absolute best thing you can do for your newborn (at the hospital) is … to **NEVER** separate from them, and keep them, skin-to-skin on your chest … meaning, placing your naked baby on your naked chest. This increases circulation, regulates temperature and regulates hormones, said Ms Gibson. She adds that stress chemicals are being released every time the baby leaves its mother for various procedures and the visitors that want to hold them. All babies require the close rhythms of their caregiver, as with skin-to-skin, in order to properly develop the chemical connections that regulate hormones, circadian rhythms and neurotransmitters. Ms. Gibson adds that colic and sleep issues can be resolved with skin-to-skin care.

*****I believe skin-to-skin can even be used to settle babies beyond the first few weeks and months, but through their first year of life. It's not something I specifically knew about when my daughter was a baby, though I recognize how helpful more of it would have been.

Further things to keep in mind …

Supportive Care: If you feel that a hospital birth is in the best interest of your family, it's worth consulting with a midwife and/or doula, to gain the widest array of choices that match what your baby needs. There are also birth centers and midwives in hospitals, which can provide a beautiful blend of care. Also, the support of a childbirth educator, trained as a doula, is associated with positive outcomes including shorter labors, less epidurals, less Pitocin administration (induction) and a significant reduction in cesarean birth (Trueba, G. et al., 2000).

Birth plan, provider and location choice/instinct: Listen to your baby (which is the union of your intuition) in creating a birth plan (a written plan of what you want your provider to do or not do). Listen to that instinct when making a choice of a birth center, a particular hospital or to be at home. You may have an instinct to choose a particular doctor, doula or midwife. People will have lots of opinions, stick to yours. Then research your choice to find science behind what you know to be true. It's there.

Search Items: Water birth, birth center, midwife and doula. Standard hospital birth procedures, circumcision and newborn skin-to-skin benefits.

Strength in your beliefs: Know that the doctor or midwife you have drawn to assist you, is perfect for you. Help them to understand your **Gut + Research**. If they cannot appreciate your **Gut + Research**, thank them profusely for their work, and love whatever lessons you've gained (there are probably many) and move on gracefully, to a provider that matches those instincts. The intelligence of nature that makes up your pregnant mind is the primary authority. Please honor it.

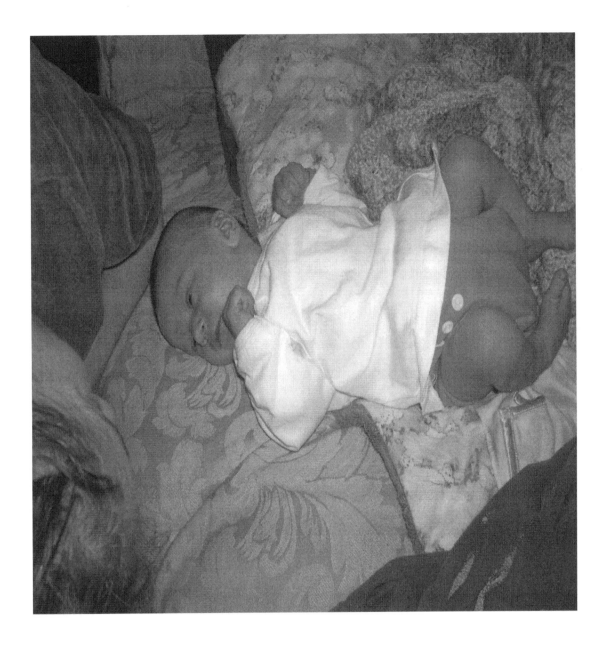

My daughter at three weeks old. A natural birth potentially means a super alert baby with a great ability to bond.

7. PLACENTA/CORD CUTTING:

Please give your baby the stem cells from the placenta: *Whatever birth location you choose be it home birth, home birth or home birth ... kidding, hospital or birth center whatever guide you choose to support what you're doing, be it midwife, midwife or midwife ... kidding, doula or doctor, please don't cut the cord of the placenta until at least! one hour, but preferably (by my recommendation) 24 hours has passed since the birth of your baby (or better yet, let the cord fall off naturally). The placenta is pumping enough iron and protein in your baby for the next month, as well as extra nutrient-rich blood and stem cells. In fact, the concentration of stem cells is the highest in fetal blood when compared to stem cell concentration at any other point in life, because of the high concentration of stem cells in the placenta* (Mercer, JS, Erickson-Owens, DA, 2012).

Placenta stem cells become radial glia that become astrocytes (your control panel or motherboard): Stem cells can become new astrocytes, glial cells and neurons when needed, like when there has been trauma to the brain, or when one is learning new more complex tasks/information (Castillo, M., 2009). Research indicates that stem cells become radial glial cells and then move into astrocytes (www.nature.comneuro/journal/v6/n11/full/nn144.html) and you know I can't say enough about how important the astrocytes are! In delaying cord cutting, you will know that the placenta (filled with stem cells) begins the progression of stem cells to radial glia for your embryo and the longer your just born baby remains connected to its stem cell initiator, the more stem cells your baby gets. Then the easier it is for your baby to heal or become a super genius and the easier it will be for your baby, grown to adult, to stay well and become well faster. **Note:** I just learned from a pregnant mother, that Yale New Haven Hospital delays cord clamping. Go Yale!!! Doctors, providers and hospitals, please, please join Yale and wait to cut the cord of the placenta.

In the article, *Rethinking placental transfusion and cord clamping issues,* it acknowledges the need to change the hospital procedure of cutting the cord immediately:

> Delay of cord clamping substantively increases iron stores in early infancy. Inadequate iron stores in infancy may have an irreversible impact on the developing brain despite oral iron supplementation. Iron deficiency in infancy can lead to neurologic issues in older children, including poor school performance, decreased cognitive abilities and behavioral problems. The management of the umbilical cord in complex situations is inconsistent between birth settings. A change in practice requires collaboration between all types of providers who attend births (Mercer, JS, Erickson-Owens, DA, 2012).

ABC news posted a story by Gillian Mohney in April of 2013 titled *New Birthing Trend, Don't Cut the Cord.* The article indicated that "umbilical non severance" is becoming more of a trend in western culture. The placenta is really a part of the baby and the article indicated that the baby is made out of the same cells. I will add that this practice is not just about health benefits; the placenta is the baby's connection to the mother and thought by some cultures to be traumatic for the baby when it is abruptly cut. This life giving force (also called the Tree of Life) is sacred ... give your baby time biologically, mentally and emotionally to let it go.

Tree of life: When the placenta is birthed and placed on a white piece of paper, the blood makes a picture of a tree from the patterned lines on the placenta, hence its reference to the tree of life. The placenta is something to be honored here, both biologically and spiritually, not abruptly cut from the baby, quickly thrown away and never seen by the mother.

Lotus Birth: Some people (when I say some, I mean not that many, but we can change that!) have what's called a lotus birth where the placenta remains attached to the belly button until it falls off naturally, between three to five days after birth. Babies who have this experience are thought to be calm, clear, with a strong sense of self and well-being. Having had a lotus birth with my daughter, I so completely recommend it. It's not easier, but it's a beautiful experience, that I think really matters. When you research it, you will learn that the placenta has to be treated and cared for, to be properly kept alongside your newborn. Things are very slow while maneuvering your baby with an attached placenta. I think those first days are meant to be very, very quiet. It's really, really lovely. The placenta honestly felt like something still living alongside my daughter. **Note:** I am hoping that things have advanced since 2008, because when I told people I was having a lotus birth and what it entailed, I might as well have said, "I am raising my daughter among elephants so that she will absorb their calm strength and intelligence" (Gosh, that's not a bad idea!). I found myself restricting the whole "I am birthing my daughter, then the placenta and leaving the two attached for a few days" because as I was strong in pregnancy, I was also a little vulnerable. Don't be afraid to restrict any information about your decisions with people who will raise their eyebrows, laugh at you, or criticize. Intelligent, ignorant people are the worst because they think they have a right to trample on your progressive knowledge simply because it is foreign to their experience. Don't let them!

Do I think the lotus birth made a difference in who my daughter is today? I do. People have always commented on my daughter's soulful nature and have said that she is wise beyond her years. She can be a totally regular type of kid, and she can also very accurately intuit the nature of things and people. She can have a stimulating conversation with any adult, and knock your socks off with her otherworldly type knowledge. Let me give you some examples …

My daughter says things like, "I am working on healing my back because I hurt it in a past life" or "Mom, you have a childhood memory stuck on your arm, do you want me to heal it?" She has talked about Mother Mary and Jesus as her familiars and said at age four in conversation about the spirit world, something about herself with "big boy Jesus." She has started more than a handful of stories with, "When I lived with Mother Mary." I had no Bibles in my home and really didn't talk about Christian themes. Not that I don't like Bibles or Christian themes exactly. I grew up Catholic, but have not been practicing since my early twenties. I have always been "spiritual" with an eclectic mix of what I feel it means to connect to something greater. Anyway, we now have three Bibles in our home, a statue of Mother Mary, a statue of Buddha, angels, angel cards and some Goddess books. Once when at a bookstore, my daughter was given a choice of books to buy, she chose a child's Bible and has now read it cover to cover dozens, literally dozens of times. (I don't think a lotus birth means your child will be interested in Bibles but I believe it could keep them tapped into what they need for their spiritual health.) **Note:** Finding ways to connect to this aspect of self is truly important. (Please see the later section on the spiritual self of your child.)

For the past four years, my daughter has talked about going to "Night School" when she goes to bed and has said that she provides me with information (that she gets at Night School) about the brain for my clients. "Night School" is reported by her to be completely amazing, filled with super smart spirit guides, beautiful things like winged fairy wolves, hummingbirds and so on. She frequently references "her librarian" when spouting information that she's learned about the earth, the body, the brain and so on. One night, as my daughter lay next to me in bed, she said, "I'm off to Night School" and I said, "OK, I love you, have a great time." She closed her eyes and then after 20 seconds went by she opened her eyes, looked around and said, "Oh, I'm still here!" I replied, "Well, close your eyes again, just give it a minute, you'll get there." She said recently, "I have been grumpy for weeks and my guide (a large name that I can't remember) has been helping my brain with this at Night School." Another night, she said that they built a bridge with an eye in the center. She asked me if I wanted a bridge, "yes" I replied. She then said, "Do you want a bridge with a heart in the middle or an eye in the middle? The heart is for love and the eye is to see the future." Hmm … the eye … maybe she is talking about the pineal gland?

My daughter says that she not only visits Night School, but the spirit world as well. She sometimes talks to plants, says Buddha is a woman and may refer to herself as the last goddess from time to time. Now, she certainly has parents that are into all this kind of stuff, but most of this has been generated by who she is. Every child has this deep connection to soul and self if they don't' become biologically clouded and if they are honored for what they know. I believe that the lotus birth means your child does not separate from the energy they were created from.

Now, don't get me wrong, my seven year old sometimes talks to me like a teenager, loves Fancy Nancy, riding a scooter and wearing fashionable things. She seems to be keenly aware that not everyone talks to each other about spiritual sorts of stuff and will hush me if I venture into those topics outside of our personal realm. Anyway, while my child is acculturated to social norms (in a mostly good way) she is very connected to a deep spiritual aspect of herself. **Note:** I am aware that as my daughter grows, that acculturation is becoming more interesting than looking at angel cards with her mother. I also know that the foundation of spirit that sourced from her lotus birth will always be with her and may be something she comes back to throughout her childhood and more deeply as an adult.

Tip to Consider: If you decide on doing the full lotus birth, rather than just the delay in cord cutting, be sure to research the proper care of the placenta, and care of the cord. Um, I apparently did not do enough prep! While my daughter's placenta was just fine (salted, with herbs and wrapped), the actual cord wrap we made, came off. The cord hardened into an arch. You can imagine the challenge in maneuvering a newborn with the placenta still attached by a brown inflexible rainbow (the cord). It was causing my daughter some discomfort and so on day four we (the baby daddy and I) cut the cord instead of letting it fall off naturally. It was done lovingly and mindfully, with an intention to keep my daughter connected to the power of this life sustaining part of her. For the next couple of days, the unattached wrapped placenta was kept close to her, something she hugged while sleeping on her side, in continuance of its important physical and spiritual role.

Search Items: The benefits of lotus birth and delayed cord cutting. Lotus birth children.

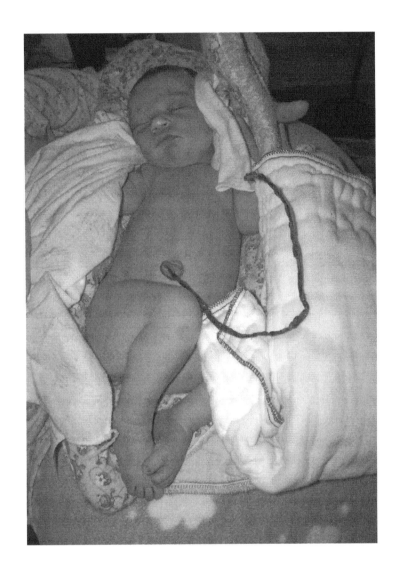

Lotus Birth of my daughter.

8. VISITATION:

In some Native American cultures only the mother and father were present with the baby at birth and for the following two weeks. This was thought to secure the bond between the baby and its parents in a calm and restful state. For me, pregnancy and beyond, converted my central nervous system into the Grizzly bear mother, "don't you come near my cub, or I will literally take you down," sort of system. Suddenly, I was very molecularly aware of what and who was crossing paths with my newborn, infant and child. Anyway, consider limiting your visitors post birth and spacing visitation.

Your baby has an energy field that is a living, molecular structure of cells that interact with people and the environment. The newborn's energy field (**and not yet developed blood-brain barrier**) requires consideration and protection (as does your infant, toddler and young child, lessening to a degree as they grow). If you tune to this, you will feel it and know just what to do. Consider telling people that you're keeping things low-key and that you'd love to schedule a visit when things settle in. They might be initially a little offended however your baby's field of energy is yours to watch over. Protecting your baby and loving your family can coexist. Having separate meaningful visits instead of the parade of guests that typically come on the first day is the best you can do for your baby (in my opinion) and can actually keep newborns from being exposed to bio-toxins in overload. I don't recommend that you tell your Great-Aunt Bertha that her bio-toxicity levels represent a direct threat to your baby's well-being. It would be said more like, "No, no, we love you, we're just going to settle in before we have visitors."

I had no visitors until a week after my daughter was born and, truth be told, was cared for by the baby daddy. I know you're thinking, "what went wrong with the baby daddy, he seems like a progressive, nice guy." Deep breath. Twenty more deep breaths. Alright, alright … I thank you baby daddy for caring for me at a very important time and supporting all of my decisions. On with it. We spent this extraordinary time playing beautiful music, singing, praying and being quiet. I spoke with my daughter often about my intention to honor her through her life. When the week had passed special visits with my mother and father, then my siblings and other loving family and friends were spaced out over the following week to keep the birth space quiet and as a sanctuary for my newborn. These visits meant so much to me and I was able to truly enjoy the company.

Special Note: When the baby is passed from person to person, the baby is away from its mother which could create biological stress to the newborn. Everything that happens in the first year of life means something to the baby's forming biology. Additionally, giving your infant absolute comfort means internalized comfort and well-being that they will express in themselves, throughout their lives.

First few weeks: When your baby is born to you, it is the greatest miracle. Treasure this brief time as if everything about the kind of relationship you will have with your child, depends upon how you spend the first days, the first few weeks. I believe there is truth in this.

9. EXTENSTION OF THE WOMB:

A newborn's central nervous system continues to develop in the three months following birth and beyond, requiring an incredible amount of support from the physical closeness of mother or primary caregiver whose rhythms strongly assist the baby's biological rhythms (www.parentmap/baby'sfourthtrimester). In other cultures, where women carry their babies on them all day long, breastfeed all through the day and sleep with their babies on top of them, there are little to no colic issues or difficulty with soothing or excessive crying (www.parentmap.com/article/babys-fourth-trimester-helping-your-baby-make-a-peaceful-transition-from-womb-to-world). Even if your baby has none of the above mentioned issues, such as colic, keeping them close still means something important to their developing biology and lifelong emotional strength.

Search Item: Please check out **The Happiest Baby on the Block**, by Harvey Karp, which details information about the fourth trimester or the first three months of life. *****Also, please research baby's central nervous system (CNS) development during the first three months (they really need the mama or primary caregiver to biologically emulate CNS functions, by closeness).

Stay close to home (pretty please) if you can: The first three months are a very important time to assist your baby to adjust to the world. Stay close to home, pretty please if you can. Make a beautiful cave and keep that baby in it. Whenever possible, please keep newborn babies from grocery stores or other high traffic, high energy situations … it is sincerely too much for them. I know there are other children to think about, single parents who have to eat and so on, but whatever you can do to keep the nest small and quiet, close to home is best. Babies who spend their time in this way, will have happier dispositions. They won't have to feel irritated by all that energy they have to sort through in the outside world. Naturally, they will sleep better, bond better, eat better and so on. When you do have to go out with your newborn, super, super please *__wear them in a baby sling__*, close to the breast, and keep an intention of well-being around them (a baby love covenant). If you are able to be out in nature, awesome! ... free, pure, clean energy absorbing into your baby's cells (see more in coming paragraph). **Note:** I know that many families don't have the luxury of staying home for three months because of jobs and the needs of other children. You can only do the best you can in the context of your life situation. It's all OK, it really is (but … please ask the caregiver to wear your newborn in a baby sling, through at least the first three months).

Search Items: Baby Slings!!!!

Pineal gland rhythms and closeness: OK, let's take the previous paragraphs from a pineal gland circadian rhythm perspective. I imagine that the pineal gland rhythms and gene code expressions (please refer back to pineal gland section) will learn a strong circadian rhythm by very, very close proximity to an already developed circadian rhythm, sort of like how entrainment works in music. I imagine that a pineal gland alone could feel confused and a little bit lost and could then make confused and lost rhythms. I imagine that a pineal gland learning rhythm in high energy situations in the outside world will learn some chaotic rhythms. I imagine that a pineal gland in a quiet home rhythm will have a chance to focus on what needs to be developing internally (rather than managing hectic external rhythms). Please, please keep newborns on your body and rarely take them off (most especially if out of the home). *****Well, with one exception ... consider pineal gland rhythms possibly disrupted by a radiation releasing cell phone. If you can, have your partner or close loved one hold your newborn/infant when you need to use the cell phone or ... install a pay phone in your home.

No sleep training: Newborn specialist Ms. Gibson stated that, if you're considering sleep training, it does not occur in the first three months of life. I have co-slept through my daughter's early childhood, and, honestly, up until about a minute ago (see Sleeping Environments). So, I might tag on a few more months and years to that three month mark.

SPECIAL NOTE: Internal security is not something a newborn baby (or infant or toddler) should be learning by being taught to adjust to situations, like sleeping alone or being exposed to people or circumstances, so they can get used to it. Babies are not learning lessons appropriate to older children. Security and well-being are internalized in a newborn (or infant or toddler) by experiencing absolute security and well-being. Then, when it's time for them to learn lessons as an older child, they will have inside them what it truly takes to own that lesson with confidence.

Newborn pace: When I was adjusting to newborn life, there were times of feeling intense anxiety (please see later sections on emotions and healing them). When you step into the newborn's world it is so different from what everyone else is doing. Eating and sleeping at weird times, it throws you off, undoubtedly. The adjustment can feel very uncomfortable at first, like you've been left in the cave alone. Once you realize that the newborn stage is short, in the scheme of things, the cave can actually be peaceful and beautiful. The pace of American culture is in us, and when we slow down so dramatically, there can actually be guilt. Identify it when you feel it, then throw it out. Slow and quiet is the best you can give your newborn. With that said, there are a multitude of situations, circumstances, work and other children. We can only do the best we can.

Being in nature: Even though I'm recommending that you stay close to home, getting out of the house can sometimes be essential for your well-being. It was and is for mine. Nature is a molecular restart button when infants, toddlers and beyond, seem out of balance. You may notice throughout the book that I am like ... go, go got your back nature's cheerleader and well, because I am. So ... another plus for nature besides just being amazing ... woods, rivers, oceans, gardens and mountains have high levels of negative ions, which can bring a feeling of calm and well-being and can reduce the effects of exposure to electromagnetic fields (EMFs). **Side note:** The effects of EMFs and cell phone radiation on newborns, infants and children needs to be more thoroughly researched. Please see what you can find. I believe it's causing problems with glial cells, overstimulating them to trigger cortisol production, which could show up as sleep problems, possibly health problems and hyperactivity. (see section on television/cell phone exposure). Additionally, there is a popular misconception that we need to stimulate the heck out of children when in actuality nature is the kind of stimulation that connects centered, grounded intelligence. Lastly on this topic, anxiety in you makes anxiety in baby. Nature helps bring peace to both.

Emotions recording: Your feelings, thoughts and conversations are being recorded by your newborn and infant. Please keep things as uplifting and jovial as possible. (This is not always easy and I was no master at this.) Stress, parent arguing and anxiety are brain imprinted by your little one. Be strong. Stay Positive! *******Also, please consider what you are ingesting through media, news and movies. For anyone in your household, please, please give up violent video games and crime shows as soon as conception. Your infant can not tolerate harsh information (please see the section on television exposure). What parent ingests, embryo/infant/child ingests.**

10. BREASTFEEDING:

The perfect food: Everybody's heard it … breastfeed your baby! and I will add for the first two years of your child's life (at minimum). Breast milk is nature's most nutrient dense, perfect food, with a biologically specific formula made for your baby. Nature is so amazing ... baby born, food included. Not only is mother's milk a formula of biological perfection, the act of a baby sucking on their mother's breast makes brain connections. I hypothesize that breastfeeding puts the baby's astrocytes and glial cells in direct connection to the mother's astrocytes and glial cells. This cell to cell bonding is how I believe entrainment of love occurs. Great bonus reasons for breastfeeding … it's free and no mixing powders in the middle of the night.

The Europeans breastfeed their toddlers, why don't we?: While breastfeeding toddlers are more commonly seen in European countries (and frankly, all over the world), it is becoming *somewhat?* more normalized in the United States. <u>In the most formative years of brain development, giving baby and toddler the best, most nutrient dense food is going to make a child who has access to their highest state of intelligence and emotional wellbeing.</u> In fact, the miraculous breast milk, changes its formula as your child grows to specifically meet the very important brain developments that happen at each phase of growth …and hey, the Europeans are doing it! Plus, being able to soothe the sometimes roller coaster emotions of a toddler with some loving breast milk is a major plus. Breastfed toddlers are sick less often and when they do get sick, it's with much less severity. Along with strengthening your loving beautiful bond, extended breastfeeding is possibly the greatest way to create an environment in which your body chooses healthy genetics. Breastfeeding is the best food on the planet. Give more.

*****Speaking of best food and biologically specific formula from the breast … my sister Jennifer used one breast for her toddler and the other breast for her infant. The infant's milk was a bluish white and the toddler's milk from the other breast was thicker and yellowish white. AMAZING!

Progressive women extend breastfeeding into toddlerhood: There is still some ignorance about extended breastfeeding in the United States, even though The World Health Organization recommends two years of breastfeeding, at minimum. Our popular culture has fed the notion that mothers who extend breastfeeding have something askew in their constitution, making them emotionally needy. The truth is most women who extend breastfeeding are intelligent, well-read, progressive people. When I was breastfeeding my daughter (until the age of three), I was surrounded by a culture of women pretty much doing the same. So I rarely felt the self-consciousness that many American women may feel in making the choice to extend breastfeeding.

When my daughter was four, I was at a party of not-so-open-minded folks, lovely, but not open-minded. It somehow came up that I breastfed my daughter until the age of three. There was a gasp, everyone went silent, and then, looked at the floor. One woman said out loud, "I don't like that. I don't think that's right." I simply responded, "It's the best food on the planet, I wanted to give her as much of it as I could." My daughter is better for it, having more resources emotionally, cognitively and physically, that make a lifelong difference. Stay strong. At the end of the day, your child will be healthier, more intelligent and more emotionally secure than they would be without it. Enough said.

Strut your breastfeeding toddler stuff!: A massive contribution to the planet could be given by going out in public and allowing others to witness the beauty of you breastfeeding your toddler. Maybe you want to throw on your best hippy dress or a three inch pair of vegan red stilettos, a pencil thin, calf length, organic cotton skirt and Mineral Fusion mascara (Mineral Fusion – great natural make-up company), whatever you like, get yourself out there. Show other women and families what it means to confidently give your child the best food/medicine on the planet. If someone gives you an uneasy look, tap your red vegan stiletto on the sidewalk and smile … NOW they know different.

SPECIAL NOTE: If you are considering formula, please don't, unless there is a serious complication in which you cannot breastfeed. I'd like to throw back in … seriously no judgment about whatever you decide. Sometimes stress, is enough of a reason to stop breastfeeding. Though I will add, breastfeeding helps produce all of those love chemicals in you, which actually reduce stress. Your child will likely have less behavior and health problems because of long-term breastfeeding, so again, less stress (plus, your boobs look so good!). If you do stop breastfeeding, please, please, please research organic non-dairy, non- gluten formulas or, even better, look into breast milk donors, they exist. **Note:** If there is a problem with breastfeeding such as difficulty latching on, ask your doctor or naturopath about tongue tie (when the tongue is anchored to the mouth). Tongue tie can also be associated with mouth breathing, difficulty sleeping and even ADHD (Thank you APRN Nicole Casbarro and Dr. Lopusny for this information).

Unhealthy infant formula: I randomly received a free sample of infant formula in the mail. It was made of cow's milk and has gluten in it, which are typically very difficult for infants and young children to digest. It is then loaded with other unidentifiable (to me) chemicals and ingredients. The fact, that I received newborn formula in the mail as a solicitation for use is discouraging to our culture. Pushing the sampling of formula doesn't help infants, and it gives people the idea that there could be a choice in what to feed your baby. A little booklet was included in the sample that talked about the importance of breast milk. It then displayed pictures of a seven or eight month-old infant weaning onto formula.

Baby Twinkie or baby avocado: I know this is repetitious, but so important … if there is no serious medical or mental health reason, please do not switch from the best, most nutrient-dense food on the planet! during the most important year of life to something that can actually cause health problems. Anyway, it's like saying … we are going to wean off your lunchtime avocado, and replace it with a Twinkie. Did I mention that even the act of a baby sucking on its mother's breast, (as opposed to pumped breast milk, which we sometimes have to do) makes very important brain connections? The good news is that within the western medical community, everyone pretty much agrees that breastfeeding is the absolute best a baby can get. Matching The World Health Organization's two year breastfeeding recommendation is the next step and would mean children who have the absolute best chance at healthy genetic expression. Remember, the best way to choose healthy genetics is to create an environment where the glial cells are performing optimally, and breast milk is one of the most important ways that this can be achieved.

Search Item: The Benefits of Extended Breastfeeding. La Leche (Breastfeeding/Mother Support) *www.lllusa.org*

Formula company message: **Dear formula company, I have a loving idea for you.** *__Take the billions of dollars you have made and start a campaign for extended breastfeeding in America. Then over the next fifty years, you may have repaired the damage you have done to the mental and physical health of humanity.__* **You could also create a formula that includes coconut milk, coconut oil, coconut butter and spirulina, which are superfoods and most closely emulate breast milk (to be used only in extreme cases like when a mother is sick or something). Please don't add much else, you don't need it … but with every ethical fiber of your being, I will say again, please encourage extended breastfeeding as number one! Thank you, you love children, want the best for them and do not need an addition on your third house. I want the best for them too and would like just one house.**

Unhealthy Supplements for Infants and Children: Please, please read the labels of common infant and child supplements also meant to promote weight gain or improve nutrition?! Like the infant formula, some are filled with gluten, dairy and canola oil, plus chemicals and other unidentifiable (to me) ingredients. It's like fried chicken grease mixed with a fast food vanilla milkshake and just a hint of vitamin B12. Yum! Please research the effects of canola oil on the body, especially if it is genetically modified (it is if doesn't say nonGMO, the oil is probably genetically modified).

*****Whenever you stop breastfeeding, hopefully never or when your child is fourteen (totally kidding), please consider superfoods such as spirulina and coconut products (as said above), which have similar nutritional components to breast milk. I know I tend to repeat myself, forgive me.

Ritual for ending extended breastfeeding: I know women who blissfully breastfeed their babies and never wanted to stop. Others of us struggle more with the physical demands of it. I was both blissful and struggling, at times. When my daughter was three years, two months of age, I was ready to end the demand on my body (though my daughter would have happily gone on longer). We talked about transitioning well beforehand, framing it as a rite of passage. She was on board, until the first night of no breastfeeding, in which she cried and cried, seemingly worried about the loss of this connection to mama. It was very, very, hard for both of us. While she was crying, I reminded her that the next day we would be having a big celebration about letting go of breastfeeding. I asked her how she wanted to celebrate, and through her tears and sobs, she said, "I want a cake and … I want red tulips." So the following day, that is just what we did (cake and tulips) for what we called "The red tulip party."

Making a ritual for your little one to transition out of this important stage or other stages, is a strong way of honoring their feelings and bringing them successfully into their next phase of life. I would love for you to buy tulips and call your ritual "The red tulip party" so that my daughter could be responsible for a mass movement. No pressure. Anyway, a dear friend celebrated this transition by having a weaning party for her daughter and many families with breastfeeding toddlers celebrate in this way. My friend explained that her daughter wanted to kayak with her father and so on the day of weaning she had her first ride, sailing off into her new beginning. OK, so I am little dramatic, but nice story, right?

11. SLEEP ENVIRONMENTS:

Co-sleep strengthens an infants' central nervous system: Hormones and neurotransmitters are produced and firing in a baby's brain during physical touch and closeness by their mother, primarily, but also by the baby's father and possibly other caregivers, thereby strengthening the developing central nervous system (babyreference.com/bonding-matters-the-chemistry-of-attachment/). For this reason and others, please consider doing research on the benefits of physical closeness and co-sleeping. Please look into the concepts of attachment parenting and the how to of sleeping next to your baby (always co-sleep on a bed or other flat surface). Our unknown adult fears can come from these early moments and years. When the baby sleeps alone in their own room, they could be experiencing fear until a parent awakes and gets to them. A baby forms brain connections based on some foundation of feeling scared, rather than nurtured closely next to mother, where they feel continually calm and secure, producing all those good hormones and neurotransmitters. We can possibly eradicate, at least a few adult issues in our children, by the simple measure of sleeping near our babies.

In the article, *Why Babies Should Never Sleep Alone: A Review of the Co-Sleeping Controversy in Relation to SIDS, Bedsharing and Breastfeeding,* it indicates that mothers who co-sleep report less infant crying, increased milk supply and improved infant sleep (McKenna, J. and McDade, T., 2005). When infants sleep in the same room with the caregiver, Sudden Infant Death Syndrome (SIDS) is reduced, and the article states, that most SIDS has primarily occurred when the infant is sleeping alone (McKenna, J. and McDade, T. 2005). Solitary infant sleep and bottle feeding became a trend in the 1950s and "good babies" became ones that slept alone and through the night (McKenna, J. and McDade, T. 2005). This trend has possibly damaged the psychology of some mothers who feel that they're failing as parents, because their babies are waking periodically through the night (McKenna, J. and McDade, T. 2005).

Biologically, infants are not designed for this 1950s mentality since their nighttime waking, crying and feeding cycle supports the physical demands of their development (McKenna, J. and McDade, T. 2005). This cultural paradigm has possibly contributed to generations of people forced to suppress their biological needs in infancy, rendering them adults who feel guilty for listening to their natural rhythms.

Some parents may feel absolutely uncomfortable with the co-sleep, and so, instead, buy a small crib that attaches to their bed, so that baby is nice and close. You have to do what's right for you, but it's worth understanding the beneficial effects on a baby's development by sleeping close. This decision could mean the difference between a regulated, happy baby and an irritable, tense baby. This decision could mean the difference between a well-adjusted, content adult and an adult who suffers from unidentifiable feelings of anxiety and depression. It could mean that much.

Claim the connection to your baby: If at the beginning, babies feel as secure as possible, there's a good chance that they will be more self-assured, kinder people because they will have internalized what it means to be safe. They will not be forced to be emotionally or physically alone, something that babies are not biologically ready for. No other mammal leaves their infant alone, putting a newborn baby monkey down to sleep at north bush while mommy monkey sleeps alone in south bush. In the past, we wouldn't either. If we saw footage of an infant monkey alone, we would likely weep (unless you are a cold, unfeeling, selfish pig ... ok, throw the book down, I'm kidding, I'm kidding!). We have become so desensitized, that when we see newborns lined up alone in square hospital cribs, we consider this normal. As parents, we need to take back this connection to our children. It is ours!

Co-Sleep on flat surface: If you choose to co-sleep, please be sure that you and baby are on a flat surface (no couches) and please! be sure that both parents or any adult sleeping in the bed (no weirdoes please), have not, been using any kind of drugs (even some pharmaceutical drugs), or have ingested heavy amounts of alcohol (if you are breastfeeding, lay off the sauce, although a little beer is said to bring in that magic milk). Please consult with a doctor about the type of pharmaceutical you or upstanding other is prescribed, with questions about the level of sedation, particularly sleep aids, pain killers or psychotropic medication. This could interfere with the natural instincts to wake before rolling into the space where your child is co-sleeping. Also, please consider putting one side of the bed up against a wall and then walling the other side with heavy pillows. This will ensure that your child does not roll off the bed when old enough. Please research safety procedures in co-sleeping.

Search Item: Check out Sobakawa pillows, very heavy pillows made of buckwheat. My daughter was sandwiched between them, so she couldn't roll off the bed and no one (me or baby daddy) could roll on her. Baby Daddy gets credit for the sperm as said earlier, the Sobakawa ... and, OK, a few more things!

Easy access to breast milk: Aside from all the comfort and closeness of co-sleeping, your baby has ready access to that super-nutrient breast milk. Often my daughter did not wake up fully because she was drinking my breast milk before she could. I never had to get out of bed and the two of us returned to sleep almost immediately. Not always, but a lot. So that's an awesome, immediate benefit.

Co-sleep for toddlers and beyond: Sleeping next to your children can be so beautiful, even through toddlerhood and beyond. Research tribal and family beds please. As stated above, children who have this level of comfort and security internalize that level of comfort and security. If co-sleeping is not for you, consider lying next to your child rubbing their back and telling them a story until they fall asleep. When children are scared, they are really and truly having an experience of fear. The biological responses to fear occur in real or imagined events. Until children are age six or older, they need you to help them handle their fear by being near them and to view the reality of the situation, i.e. no monsters in the closet. You will not spoil or ruin them, quite the opposite. You will strengthen them.

Early security means strength in adults: In my work as a therapist, I come across many adults, who, when asked about their early childhood, get a sick feeling in their stomach. They were afraid as children, and their adult anxieties link back to a lack of security. Generations of people have been pushed at a very young age to be independent about basic needs, primarily sleeping by one's self. We have been led by culture to believe that if your baby or child sleeps on their own, you've succeeded and that if they sleep with you, you've failed or worse, there is something wrong with your family. This is simply, not true.

Search Items: Co-sleeping and Attachment Parenting.

Special story: I co-slept with my daughter up until three days ago (this paragraph was written on the eve of my daughter's seventh birthday 10/24/15.) I honestly cannot say enough about how beautiful it has been to cuddle up with my daughter at bedtime, at morning time or to read with a low light next to my growing, sleeping beautiful girl. It's where we've talked about the most important things, beliefs and ideas. I wouldn't trade it for anything. Tears welling. Tears welling. **Note**: Please know that co-sleeping occurs in all kinds of family situations and is not dependent upon someone being single (regardless of my status, it is what I believe is best). Most co-sleeping families that I know are married couples with children. Please do not allow anyone to construe this practice as a parent's neediness which is a common cultural projection. In true attachment/co-sleeping intention, parents use this practice with instinct, intelligence and research to provide their child nurturance, love and total security in childhood. It is also OK and very beautiful for a healthy parent to love sleeping near their child or children. There are cases when the practice is not a well thought out practice, but an actual issue of enmeshment or a parent emotional issue. Parents please evaluate your position or work with someone who can help you evaluate your position, so that a co-sleeping practice is for the highest and best good for your children. (That someone may not be a typical psychotherapist who may go straight to co-sleeping means enmeshment.)

With that said, I began angling my daughter's sleep-in-her-own-bed scenario, several months before the actual event. At one point in this unpopular preparation, my daughter said, "You can't force me to sleep in my own bed, I'm not ready." It was more like my daughter screaming, "You can't force me. You can't force me." I can only imagine what my landlord (who lives on the other side of our thinly walled apartment) was thinking. So, we agreed upon practicing, starting in my daughter's room with story and such, and then coming into mine ... a mock sleep in own bed. We didn't always stick with the practice, but it still set the ground for psychological change. The week before my daughter's seventh birthday, she announced that she was ready for her own room and she did it just like that. (Except that two days later she was ready to come back. So, we made a sleep-next-to-mommy once-a-week rule that grew into twice-a-week rule.) I explained that while I truly missed her, I still have to send her off to college and in this case, off to her own bed.

The first night, ALONE, I sat in my king bed, drinking an Amstel Light (yes, I know, not gluten-free, not organic, it was in the fridge left by previous tenant ... sorry I do all kinds of hypocritical things that you likely won't do) thinking that I felt sad. I launched into thoughts about how maybe I missed out on her childhood, didn't do enough and so on. Beware of this, it's just not healthy (and your children feel it). So, I regrouped and then tapped into the triumph of it all and how much I like my big king bed! The next morning I bought my daughter red tulips to bring ritual to this rite of passage (as we had done with the end of breastfeeding).

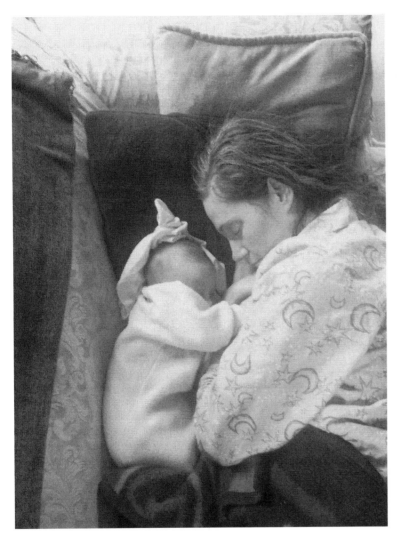

Sleeping so sweet, BUT we are on
a couch (must be a flat surface!).
We usually slept on a bed.

12. VACCINE /NATURAL IMMUNIZATION:

OK, this is a big topic. I will tread less than lightly and say things that could get your pediatrician to fire you. (Hopefully, your pediatrician is super cool and progressive, and so then they won't.) Let's just take a deep breath and repeat, "Everything is just fine. There are other pediatricians out there who won't fire me for making my own choice for my child's health, for my child's body. I will not create an epidemic of disease in the world if I don't follow the vaccine schedule. I will not create poverty for the pharmaceutical companies. They can begin mass producing safe natural vaccines. I can decide." One more deep breath. I love you, let's go on.

Child changes after vaccines: When I was pregnant with my daughter, I listened to a mother tell the incredibly sad story about the dramatic change in her two year olds behavior directly following one of the scheduled vaccinations. Her daughter's generally sweet disposition became one of uncontrollable tantrums overnight, described by the mother, as well beyond normal two year old episodes. Following testing by a naturopath, it was discovered that the two year olds behavior was related to metal toxicity and relative to the time of behavioral change, attributed to the aluminum found in vaccines. (The National Vaccine Information Center www.nvic.org states that aluminum is a heavy metal with **known neurotoxic effects** and can be found in many of the childhood vaccines along with other potentially toxic ingredients.)

Instinct: Prior to hearing the above story, I knew that I would not vaccinate my daughter. Instinct told me that my daughter would not respond well and would suffer great loss of her abilities as a person. This woman's story confirmed and solidified my instinct. I am so grateful she was willing to share. Please listen to your instinct and share what you know with others!
Side note on religious exemption: Dear U.S. Government, please continue to honor the right to religious exemption in all fifty states. In New Jersey and in some of your other states, this right has been taken away. In New Jersey when religious exemption was removed, parents who had not vaccinated their children were forced to either pull their children from school or perform a toxic overload of vaccinations. This is extremely unhealthy for a child, unlawful and unconstitutional. My God inside me, that forms my intuition, told me "Do not vaccinate your daughter, or you will lose her, not to death but her soul to her cognition." It is my child's life and my right. No system is going to take that from me and nor should they take that from anyone. In God, We Trust.

Metal toxicity: If your child has been vaccinated and is experiencing any physical or behavioral concerns, ask a naturopath to test your child for metal toxicity. Please research metal toxicity's relationship to the brain and to physical, learning or behavioral problems. Metal toxicity is highly linked to autoimmune disorders that could emerge later in life, so even if you think your child has passed through the vaccination schedule without issue, it is still worth checking on levels of metal. If levels are high, the naturopath can work with you and your child on a detox program.

SPECIAL NOTE: Please go to the National Institute of Health's PubMed. Click the search bar. Type in pineal gland and aluminum. Research articles appear. Then go back to the pineal gland section of this book, remembering how important this gland is in human functioning. One of these NIH articles indicates that pineal gland rhythms were disturbed when sea bass' pineal gland was covered in aluminum foil (Bayarri, MJ et al, 2003). Now imagine your newborn, your infant, your child.

*****The National Institute of Health posted the article *Do Aluminum Vaccine Adjuvants contribute to the rising prevalence of Autism?* (2011). In summation ... uh, yeah!!!!

The blood-brain barrier and Autism: The blood-brain barrier (paragraph repeated from section 2) is the restraint mechanisms of cell junctions, between the blood and cerebrospinal fluid (CSF) (Sanders et al., 2012). Essentially, it is the wall that keeps unwanted molecules away from the most important parts of the brain's functioning. In the article *Barrier Mechanism in Developing Brains,* it described the infant blood-brain barrier as "leaky" which "may render developing brains more vulnerable to drugs, toxins and pathological conditions, contributing to cerebral damage and later neurological disorders" (Sanders. et. al, 2012). *I spoke with a woman regarding her adult Autistic son. She indicated that the aluminum and toxins from the infant vaccines becomes locked in the brain when the blood-brain barrier later closes. She emphatically stated that this caused Autism in her son. A mother who lost her son to who he would have been is the one to ask about the latest research. Her heart has been broken, so she's the one who has the answers.*

1 in 68 children have Autism: I rarely cry about what's going on in my life. I think something's wrong with me, because I really have had things to cry about. However, when I hear stories about children who are lost to what they would have been, I really weep. 1 in 68 children has Autism and growing says the Centers for Disease Control (CDC).

Here is a very important SEARCH ITEM: Google the diseases that vaccines prevent verses the illnesses vaccines are linked to causing, placing value on what's life threatening and what's a lifelong disability or struggle, such as infant death, Autism, developmental disorders, learning disorders, health issues, autoimmune disorders and many more. Check out Mercola.com which hosts an important article to this regard ... *The Danger of Excessive Vaccination During Brain Development.*

Emotional trauma of vaccinations: A mother was talking with her friends about her three month-old baby, who recently had her ears pierced. The mother told her friends that her daughter could not stop crying following the piercing and said, "Plus she just had her shots." The mother further said "at least she won't remember" (referring to the pain of ear piercing and shots). I have not yet heard a baby cry from ear piercing, but I've heard a baby cry from a vaccination. It's heartbreaking. Babies may not have the typical conscious memory in which they can describe events, but to say they "don't remember" fear and pain, discounts how shock and trauma, seriously affects the body.

Baby could grow up with an unconscious, unresolved memory which surfaces as an unknown adult anxiety. Fourteen years of therapy and $7000 later, they acknowledge that they don't like their mother. When really, it is not that they don't like their mother, it's that their unknowing mother put the child in an unsafe (from a baby's perspective), traumatic (from a baby's perspective) situation ... like ear piercing (sorry to dozens of cultures). The traumatized baby grown to adult, does not know to say, "Uh, Mom and/or Dad, you allowed someone to put a hole in my ear or a shot in my arm, when I barely had my central nervous system strong enough to regulate my breathing. That was traumatic, what were you thinking?" Babies and children have bodies that remember pain, which, I believe, can later become a disease, mental health issues or failed something. You will not be perfect as a parent (I am far from it) and your child may go through something painful that cannot be helped (and I believe they can heal from it), but the things that we can control (as far as pain infliction goes), I believe we should. One more time, just for good effect, babies/children remember pain!

Child goes into a physical trauma state: I believe that a child could actually go into shock when vaccinated. I certainly know that the astrocytes have moved from "all is well" homeostasis to urgency because of the pain of vaccination. Then astrocytes likely remain activated or urgent, because of all the toxins in vaccines that the body must begin working very, very hard to get rid of. Not only do toxins have a higher likelihood of negative impact because of an underdeveloped blood-brain barrier, but the blood-brain barrier may be weakened because the astrocytes have turned their attention to the immediacy of the pain and toxins (Alvarez, J., Katayama, T. and Prat, A., 2013). The younger the child or infant is, the harder the physical process is. Before my sister came to learn that she would not vaccinate her children, she had an event with her oldest son. When her six month old son was given his shots, he could not stop crying. My sister couldn't console him and remembers driving home in the car with him desperately hysterical and had to pull over the car. My nephew was likely in a physical state of trauma. Think about what it would take for you to go into a state of physical trauma, usually something really big like a terrible car accident (may you and yours always be secure and well in a car and everywhere). None of us would voluntarily put our bodies in a state of physical trauma.

Ingrained system can confuse your instinct: As you know I am promoting **Gut + Research = Highest and Best Decision** ... BUT, if the gut is so confused by a heavy ingrained system combined with fear that something could happen to your child, then it is really hard to see/feel it. I don't think that the gut, if cleared, would agree to a toxic overload into your newborn or infant or toddler or child that could potentially change who they could be in the world, physically, mentally and emotionally (immediately or down the road).

While I believe strongly against the current ingredients and procedure of standard vaccinations, I feel obligated to include the following ...

Vaccination Schedule: If you feel pressured into vaccinating your child, consider the review of alternative schedules (Or, don't feel pressure and consider work with a naturopath and the alternative natural protection/homeopathic immunization detailed in coming paragraphs). If it is not pressure and you have decided that you want to vaccinate, then please, please consider this example of an alternative vaccine schedule: https://www.lewrockwell.com/2004/12/donald-w-miller-jr-md/vaccine-nation/) by University of Washington MD, Dr. Donald Miller ....

In summary:

No vaccinations until a child is two years old.

No vaccines that contain thimerosal (mercury).

No live virus vaccines (except for smallpox, should it recur).

These vaccines, to be given one at a time, every six months, beginning at age 2:
Pertussis (acellular, not whole cell)
Diphtheria
Tetanus
Polio (the Salk vaccine, cultured in human cells)

*******Dr. Miller further states that parents should be able to choose whatever vaccine schedule they want!**

******SPECIAL RECOMMENDATION:** You do not need to play Russian roulette with the fate of your child's entire life. Consider genetic testing for your baby, because if they have the genetic code for Autism, they will likely be intolerant of the intense vaccination schedule. While I am heartily against putting toxic ingredients into any children, maybe there could be a **mandate** for genetic testing until we create new and safe vaccines. Better yet we can use alternative immunizations/disease protection already available (detailed in the coming pages) **while** we are working on the creation of new and safe vaccines.

Medical Exemption: If genetic testing indicates that your child has DNA codes, making them susceptible to Autism, or auto-immune disorders or mental health problems, the law of medical exemption could be applied. Parents, this is a way you can protect your child physically and be able to send them to school, camps and so on.

Consult with a naturopath about immunizations/vaccines: A naturopath can help you with supplements, nutrition and possibly timing of vaccines to assist your child through the process. **Side note:** When my daughter was four months old, I was approached at a bookstore by a naturopath, who said, "You didn't vaccinate your baby did you?" She said that she can always tell the difference between babies that had been vaccinated and ones that hadn't. She added that babies that had been vaccinated look drugged and less alert. This naturopath felt that vaccination should not occur until a child's blood barrier is more stable and brain development more advanced. She also suggested that families research vaccinations that are truly necessary and use age, timing of vaccines and nutrition to offset their effects.

Vaccine shedding: Please research vaccine shedding ... when children who are vaccinated release viruses in their fluids. Vaccines have weakened strains of viruses so there is not a high risk (pediatrics.about.com/od/immunizations/a/live-vaccines.htm) if you have chosen not to vaccinate and your child is in a daycare full of vaccinated others. Many vaccines include no live viruses, so there is not an issue. **Note:** With that said … at age five my daughter got the chicken pox. She likely contracted it through vaccine shedding while at her learning/daycare center, because she was not in contact with anyone who had the chicken pox. Her immunity is now established and she won't have to keep up with toxic chicken pox vaccinations into her twenties. So it ended up being OK.

Strengthen the immune system to protect if you have chosen to immunize in standard care: Using essential oils (highly concentrated immune system of plants) daily (see nutrition/supplement section for more information), organic foods, herbs and holistic supplements can help support a very strong immune system. These holistic combinations can help ease the toxic shock to your child's system should you choose to vaccinate. Please research. **Note:** Extended breastfeeding could also greatly assist recovery from the toxic shock of vaccines.

Ok big systems, let's work together, there is always a solution ...

According to the film **VAXXED: From Cover up to Catastrophe**, produced by Del Bigtree, 1 in 15,000 children had Autism in the 1970s when far less vaccines were issued and currently, 1 in 68 children has Autism. **Super please watch this movie**, which indicates that the Center for Disease Control (CDC) has hidden information about the harmful effects of vaccines. I love my country, but this is an abuse that is so ... I can't seem to find the word. Oh, I found it ... inhumane! **CDC Note:** The cover up research probably happened decades ago and all the staff after that have been flowing along with the idea that vaccines are safe, so they just kept adding more and more. The reality is current CDC staff are likely very kind and not trying to cover anything up. I am sure that they want the best for children and people. So we must be present in 2016 and say "alright, these vaccines have a good intention, but they are not totally safe, so we have to shelf them. Let's work together and come up with a new way to safely protect children from disease and in the meantime, let's use immune protection and alternative immunization approaches." **Please current CDC staff, stand up for children and say so!**

Vaccine injury a coincidence?: The U.S. Federal Government has a program called the Vaccine Adverse Event Reporting System (VAERS). The following is pulled from their site: *More than 10 million vaccines per year are given to children less than 1 year old, usually between 2 and 6 months of age. At this age, infants are at greatest risk for certain medical adverse events, including high fevers, seizures, and sudden infant death syndrome (SIDS). Some infants will experience these medical events shortly after a vaccination by coincidence.* Um, by coincidence? Someone wants to acknowledge there is a problem, without taking responsibility. It's like me saying "I'm so sorry you feel upset," after I ran over your dog. **Research study reveals major problems with vaccines:** A research study which investigated the Vaccine Adverse Event Reporting System (VAERS) database between 1990 to 2010, found that babies who receive the most vaccines tend to have higher rates of hospitalization and higher death rates and ... the younger the infant, the higher the rates (Goldman, GS & Miller, NZ, 2012). We all know that we need a new way! **Please VAERS, stand up for children and say so!**

Pharmaceutical companies please take a stand: There are mothers and fathers watching their beautiful children internally caged, banging their heads, unable to smile, unable to speak. 1 in 68 children has Autism and worsening. The other 67 children might be sick frequently, having to use frequent rounds of antibiotics, or might have a learning disorder, hearing problems, emotional outbursts or may develop a disease down the road. I believe CEOs of pharmaceutical companies need to stand up and say, "I'm not making this anymore. I refuse. It has killed and harmed children, the worst offense. I won't do it. Let's take the millions upon billions I have already made, get together with other pharmaceutical CEOS, the FDA and the CDC and make a safe formula of immunization. We have the resources to do so." **Please pharmaceutical CEOs, stand up for children and say so!**

www.fdabiologicsbloodvaccines/safety/availability/vaccinesafety.htm
FDA common ingredients in U.S. Licensed Vaccines: This site has a question and answer format about vaccine ingredients. Some of the questions are as follows: Why is aluminum in some vaccines? Why are antibiotics in some vaccines? Why is formaldehyde in some vaccines? Why are preservatives in some vaccines? Why is fetal calf/bovine serum in some vaccines? My question to the FDA is why do you think it is OK to inject these ingredients in newborns? Infants? Children? People? I just want to lovingly say to the FDA, it is really not OK to do so, if you want people to be healthy, and I know you do. Toxins, like pollution, will show up somewhere. Current vaccines are not safe. **Please FDA, stand up for children and say so!**

We should not be left with these choices:

A. Your child will possibly endure a vaccine injury if you use standard care vaccinations.
B. Your child could be sick a lot, have emotional outburst or have learning problems if you use standard care vaccination.
C. Your child could end up with a serious health issue down the road if you use standard care vaccination.
D. Your child might get a disease if you don't vaccinate using standard care vaccination.

*****I want to honor that vaccines have saved people's lives. Polio was devastating and standard immunization changed that, but the consequences of vaccinations have also been devastating. We need to come out from this rock and hard place. Let's take another leap and try some new formulas.**

Formula for new vaccine: I propose that we research a formula with healthy ingredients, one that preserves the disease naturally and allows the disease to pass through the body, enough to stimulate immunity, but not stick around. Nature gave me an idea. When I was talking a walk, I decided to pick a bunch of small white wild flowers (after asking the flowers if it was OK ... they said yes), thinking that I would make some sort of flower essence preserved in apple cider vinegar. If left on their own, these white flowers would have turned brown in a day or so. After three weeks in the apple cider vinegar, the white flowers are still white. So I got to thinking ...

The AXSS (Apple Cider Vinegar, Xylitol, Salt, Silver) pill: Disease could be preserved in a pill form with apple cider vinegar and salt, essentially pickled disease ... the antigen (the part of the vaccine that stimulates the production of antibodies). Colloidal silver is added to the pill because silver is a nontoxic antibiotic. The silver suffocates (www.quantumbalancing.com/news/cs_universal) the disease so that the vinegar preserved disease can (hypothetically) be recognized for immunity, but will not become activated in the body or lay dormant in cells. Lastly ... Xylitol is a five-carbon sugar that stimulates innate immunity (Durairaj, L et al, 2004) and could possibly act to increase the immune

response to the antigen. Maybe it could be tested by a biologist. Then I need a big institute (call me) and for starters a patent … which I now declare official in this published book. Then, I need support from the FDA and CDC. So if you are any of these, please email me … kateaset@gmail.com. Thank you sincerely.

Theory: If standard vaccines contain weakened strains of viruses that can be contagious, like vaccine shedding of the chicken pox, then I wonder if in the vaccination process these weakened strains attach to cells and possibly lay dormant. I then wonder if later in life, stress and strain or physical or emotional trauma, can trigger the dormant virus to express as a different form of disease. It is the reason that I pose colloidal silver in the formula mentioned above, so that the disease is suffocated and will hypothetically pass through the body for recognition of immunity, but not attach to cells. **Note:** If you Google vaccines cause cancer, vaccines cause lupus, vaccines cause fibromyalgia, vaccines cause multiple sclerosis, vaccines cause schizophrenia, seizures and so on, unfortunately, you will find all kinds of links to information and research.

SPECIAL NOTE: Remember this from section two …

The National Institute of Health (NIH) presented the article, *Gene Scan Shows Body's Clock Influences Numerous Physical Functions: From Immunity to Thyroid Hormones, Pineal Gland Exerts Effects on 600 Genes:*

Researchers found that the pineal gland has important influence over genetics that control inflammation, the immune response, cell adhesion, reproduction and death of cells, calcium metabolism, cholesterol production, **endothelial cells** (in blood vessels) and endothelial tissue (the tissue that lines body's organs), cytoskeleton (the inner structural material of cells), transcription (the process by which DNA sequences are converted in proteins), effects on the thyroid gland, cell signaling and hormones and copper and zinc biology(www.nih.gov/news-events/news-releases/gene-scan-shows-bodys-clock-influences-numerous-physical-functions, 2009).

Is it possible that the disturbance to the pineal gland from toxins/aluminum in vaccines causes DNA sequencing to become confused or rewritten in cases of Autism? Is it possible that because DNA makes copies, that it makes copies of viruses that lay dormant and later become diseases like cancer and autoimmune disorders? Maybe I am repeating myself all over the place, but we have to put this together … we are too smart to have not put this together. Oh, maybe we have, but vaccines are such a lucrative business like cigarette smoking, why stop now? Shade pulling way down. If I should go missing, please do rally for a thorough investigation and my daughter is to be raised by my sister Cindy and her husband TJ.

*****In a research study conducted by the Salk institute (as in Jonas Salk polio vaccine pioneer with whom I completely honor) astrocytes were found to initiate gamma oscillations which are associated with higher level thinking and memory. The research team used a virus to disable the astrocyte communication and found that gamma oscillations were dampened (Lee, H. et al, 2014). This must also be also true for children exposed to a weakened strain of virus through the vaccination process? The article further states that disruptions in gamma oscillations are associated with Autism as well as other

health issues.

*****Further, vaccines trigger an immune response which means the brain/body is focusing on fighting a disease. The brain/body is no longer focusing on growing itself during the most important years of development.

OK, let's go on. Until another natural immunization is created and issued, here is a safe possibility …

Homeopathic immunizations: Homeopathy has been used successfully for centuries to heal disease, prevent disease and cure emotional distress. According to an article posted on holisticsquid.com-homeopathic-vaccines-a-good-alternative, Homeopathy uses the same principle as vaccinations, which is "like to cure like." The article gives details about how homeopathy can also appropriately stimulate the immune system in the same way that vaccines do. The article also warns that if you Google information about this you may find a whole lot of homeopathic vaccine bashing. Look further!

Please check out www.homestudy.net/research, Natural Immunization Research, which *recognizes a study in which children who used homeopathic vaccinations were the healthiest long term, when compared to children who were vaccinated and children who were unvaccinated.* Please, please check this out and leap from there.

Celletech is a company that creates homeopathic remedies of high value. They have a Tick Bites Balance 1 formula, taken regularly through the summer, designed and well-researched to help prevent the infection of Lyme if bitten by a deer tick. Their Tick Bites Balance 2 remedy is applied when bitten by a tick, as a stronger remedy once Lyme is in the system of the body. In this manner, homeopathy could be researched thoroughly as a national or global immunization program, so that tiny beings are not being injected with disease, aluminum, formaldehyde, polysorbate 80, trition X (spermacide) or other awful ingredients that will pass through to precious parts of your child's brain and central nervous system.

SPECIAL SIDE NOTE: You could work with a homeopath and naturopath to research Celletech's Tick Bites Balance 1, which could be potentially used like a vaccine, to prevent mycoplasma infections which can be transmitted in the air and water, sometimes a co-infection of Lyme disease (please read my story about this in the section on long-term health and the blood-brain barrier). It is important to note that mycoplasmas are also associated with pneumonia, the flu, chronic fatigue syndrome and other health issues. Some of the ingredients in Tick Bites Balance 1, important to this regard, include homeopathic amoxicillian and homeopathic doses of bacterial/viral infections in the "like cures like" fashion, such as Lyme, encephalitis, mycoplasma urealyticum and rickets. Please, please investigate this.

Nosodes: Nosodes are a homeopathic treatment used during a disease condition. For example, the nosode for the flu is oscillococcinum, for diptheria is diptherinum, for tuberculosis is tuberculinum, and the one for measles is morbillinum (www.the healthyhomeeconomist.com/nosodes-homeopathic-alternative-to-vaccines/).
Dr. Nancy Malik writes an article worth reviewing titled *11 Research Studies in Support of*

Nosodes: Oscillococcus, Influenzinum, Psorinum, Carcinosinum, Tuberculinum, Bacillinum, Psneumococcus, Streptococcus, Leptospira (2011). **Please check this out.**

Search Items: Homeopathic Vaccination Schedule. Dr. Emily Kane's Homeopathic Vaccination Schedule. Homeopathic Immunization Kit.

Kate Gorman's Protection Method (Researched on one child who in her seven years, has only been to the doctor for yearly physicals, the chicken pox and a urinary issue, not infection, resolved with some TLC and natural cranberry pills.) (Keep in mind, Kate Gorman, uh me, is not a doctor or naturopath and has no credentials that warrant any official protocol recommendation, other than being a **Gut + Research** parent like you.):

1.) Child is breastfed until age three or longer.

2.) Breastfeeding mother regularly ingests coconut oil and other antiviral and antibacterial agents such as organic fruits and vegetables, superfoods (As said earlier, please look into David Wolfe's Superfood information and books), herbal teas and tinctures.

3.) Infant is rubbed daily with coconut oil mixed with safe essential oils for children such as grapefruit, orange, lavender and chamomile. Please research stronger oils such as oregano and thyme that could be diffused in the house.

4.) Breastfeeding mother daily uses stronger essential oils like sage, cinnamon, rosemary and oregano, so that breastfed baby receives the higher protection provided to every cell.

5.) When exposed to illness, breastfeeding mother ingests Bentonite Clay (binds toxins to the clay and moves out the junk) along with a strong natural antibiotic such as Golden seal or Colloidal Silver. Please research other natural antibiotics.

6.) When breastfeeding has stopped, essential oil body rub for child continues along with organic foods, superfoods for children (please research) such as chlorella, spirulina, coconut oil and raw honey (age one and older) along with antiviral and antibacterial herbal tinctures and teas for both mother and child. **Note:** Stronger essential oils such as cinnamon and sage could be tested on the feet of children older than two, for added cell protection. If it is too strong as in burning or stinging, please try in a base oil such as coconut, olive or jojoba.

7.) Please research and work with a Naturopath and Homeopath about the age and timing of homeopathic immunization. Please don't forget about the Celletech, Tick Bites Balance 1.

The health of the earth and its people: The standard vaccinations we have today, should not be a way that people stay healthy, in the place of actual ways that sustain *the health of the earth and its people* long-term. Diseases die out and there are ways to best protect people through the course of them. There are many, many, many families who are not vaccinating, using herbs, organic foods, essential oils and homeopathy to sustain true health in their children, people and the planet.

13. CELL PHONE EXPOSURE/DIGITAL MEDIA/MEDIA CONTENT:

High tech phones produce an enormous amount of radiation that can affect health: So my friends think I'm kind of a freak. I can't use certain cleaning products, will only (mostly) eat organic foods and to top it off, I get vertigo near high tech phones. In 2014, I had no texting plan and practically had a flip phone. So, one of my dear friends got me an iPhone, hoping to improve my connection to the world. Well, I was so overwhelmed, by the waves of radiation coming from the phone and all the tweets, beeps and flashes, I couldn't get anything done. The phone wanted so much of my attention, and to top it off, I felt like I was on the sinking Titanic. The feeling of vertigo, I learned, is not completely uncommon in people who upgrade to higher tech phones. So after two weeks of this, I turned in my expensive iPhone and asked the AT&T customer service dude if I could have the lowest tech phone possible. Someone said to me regarding my current phone, "Oh, don't forget your calculator." I text people now … at least.

Anyway my own experience got me thinking about babies and young children ...

Radiation Exposure: The National Cancer Institute states that cell phones emit radio frequency energy, a form of non-ionizing electromagnetic radiation, which can be absorbed by tissues in the body (www.cancer.gov/cancertopics/risk/cellphones). Consider the brain and tissues of your growing fetus, newborn, infant and child, especially in relation to their vulnerability to toxins. **Please don't use cell phones or iPads when nursing or holding infants.** The fact, that infants have an underdeveloped blood-brain barrier means that particles such as radiation and otherwise, could be entering critical parts of the brain. It means that everything forming might form in competition with the components of these toxic particles. Please think of the pineal gland and circadian rhythms, gamma oscillations and so on!

A study conducted by Zhao, T. et al. (2009), indicated that the expression of specific genes and proteins in cultured cells and in intact animals can be negatively affected by radiation exposure from cell phones. The article indicates that cell phone electromagnetic waves register between 800 to 1900 MHz and because these waves are transmitted in all directions, brain cells are at risk for damage (Zhao, T. et a, 2009). Between zero and seven, the brain and body are making the most critical choices about what genes to express affecting health, physical appearance and intelligence. It feels imperative that parents research how radiation from their cell phones and other devices can create an unhealthy environment in the brain.

SPECIAL NOTE: I have witnessed children get squirmy and whiny from using their parent's cell phones, my daughter included. **Hyperactivity and difficulty with self-regulation are other behaviors that I believe come from being in close proximity to cell phones and other devices.** If, children who are regularly exposed to high technology devices were tested for radiation levels, we would have a better connection to the impact on children. However, that seems unethical, because there is already enough research out there about cell phone radiation's link to cancer. So, I think we should act on the research already available about this environmental concern. Other countries have banned child cell phone use. Please follow their lead on this. (Remember the younger your child is, the more concern you need to have!) **Note:** If you put a cell phone near the heart of someone who has a pacemaker, the pacemaker has problems (information retrieved from CDC). Now imagine the cells, tissues and organs of your child and you, for that matter.

Radiation blanket: A father told me that **The Honest Company** sells an *anti-radiation blanket* that can be worn over the pregnant mother or can be draped directly over the baby. Maybe this blanket could be placed over the tummy, if a woman over the age of thirty-five, has to have her **one** ultrasound.

*****Please think about turning off the internet and cell phones at night. Daddy's please rock the man purse, where you keep your cell phone off your body. We care about you too! Cancer has been found on the body, exactly where the cell phone has been regularly kept.

Tip: Clay is one of the best ways to remove radiation from the body. Consider ingesting Bentonite Clay (please research use), found at Whole Foods, for about eight dollars. Also, rosemary tea, extracts or oils, are also helpful in reducing radiation in the body.

Digital Media, Electromagnetic Fields (EMFs) and Sleep: As a therapist who works with families, with young children, I have come across numerous complaints about infant/child sleep issues. I am a parent with deep, deep compassion because I had a child who would wake in the middle of the night, regularly until she was around four years of age. I believe that children are having increasingly more challenges with falling and staying asleep due to the energy emitted from electromagnetic fields (EMF) exposure from digital music and television, as well as from computers and other devices. In a study conducted by Huber R. et al., (2002), it indicated that EMFs alter the brain's blood flow during sleep and wake cycles. **Note:** Ask a school teacher if they think this is affecting focus and attention.

Digital media and glial cells: All technology has a functional way of operating, which is often very different from how nature operates and how a human operates. While this cannot be seen, it still means something to the natural world and the world of an infant, child and adult, with the greatest impact on the smallest of beings. Rob Fraboni, friend, brilliant and renowned Record Producer, and entrepreneur, alerted me to the problem of digital media and the effect on the brain and central nervous system. He explained that digital media produces rapid square waves, with multiple lines of data, while the brain produces sine waves, a series of single unbroken waves of energy, like analog waves. So I theorize that when these square waves are hitting glial cell sine waves, it's a big overload for any adult, and, for someone very young, it's much more intense. Due to this media overload, many people could be operating, at least part of the day, as if they're presidential staff in the oval office during a global emergency. The rapid square waves could theoretically move your astrocytes from a resting state to an activated one, possibly allowing unhealthy genetic expression (Gosselin et al., 2010). The digital audio waves could keep people in a state of fight or flight and for a child whose brain is developing, it could be developing in a condition of stress. Developing brains in conditions of stress may have a less effective blood-brain brain barrier (Alvarez, J., Katayama, T. and Prat, A., 2013) along with other issues such as learning problems and so on. Please research.

Search Item: Keep your eye out for Rob Fraboni (robfraboni.com) who has developed a technology that protects you from EMF problems. It is a box, but no ordinary one. This device produces electo-magnetic brain wave states of calm, optimum thinking and positive frequencies of health. It causes the brain hemispheres to sync or en-train to these waves. I can personally attest to the effectiveness of this invention! It is going to change the world!!! If you have a lot of money, call Rob and tell him you want to invest in the box. You don't have to thank me, just donate a portion of your fruitful investment to children in poverty or endangered wildlife. (If you are a famous musician or aspire to be, I recommend that you hire Rob for the production of your next album. He's the best and Keith Richards thinks so!)

*****Please check out http://microwavenews.com/, which has a nicely compiled list of articles and research about the effects of EMFs on health, DNA expression and more.

Less than fifteen minutes of media time each day: Montessori and Waldorf based education recommends no media or less than fifteen minutes of media time each day. Children who watch less television and use less electronic or other devices, can hypothetically concentrate on academic or other tasks for longer periods of time because their brains are not constantly recovering from an overload of radiation or from those digital square waves. With limited television or other devices, a child's brain can be developing in a resting state where they are making connections that support their learning. I personally have not kept to less than fifteen minutes of television per day. Sometimes it's been days even weeks in a row with no television, especially in the summer. Then some days and especially some winter days, way more than fifteen minutes. Do what you can and **check this out … http://nypost.com/2016/08/27/its-digital-heroin-how-screens-turn-kids-into-psychotic-junkies/.** Lastly, if you are going to be a media driven home (like everyone is these days), try to wait until the bulk of your child's brain is developed, between ages six and seven.

Anyway, content is another consideration.

Television/Movie Content: Whoa! That's a lot to think about. Are you starting to get the picture about why I'm a single mother, as in rarely dated in the past few years? I mean, I'm a tall, thin red-head, with decent features, sort of funny, kind … but a man comes within twenty feet of me and just senses how I would seriously restrict his television or worse, not allow one in the house … It's like a "run the other way" alarm. I bumped into a hot guy at the store the other day, and when I say hot, I mean smokin' hot. We stared into each other's eyes for a long three seconds before I said, "Hi, how are you?" Inside his mind, it was possibly like, "I'm drawn to this woman, I can't avert my gaze" and then, "Oh no, oh no, the television, the television, it's off, it's gone, help me, what's happening, where is it?" He dashes off, just when I am about to optimistically launch into my next line, "Hey, do you want to live off the grid with me?" (Oh, that's a good book for someone to write, *Raising Baby off the Grid.* Please take it and run with it, as you probably don't have a way to contact me. Seriously, just go for it!) Actually, I am a television/movie watcher, just not all the time one.

Anyhow, while media exposure has biological effects, content is another highly important consideration as content can weave itself into the psychology and personality of your child. Also, please consider what you're watching even while pregnant and holding newborns/infants. If you are choosing shows that are crime-based, violent and anxiety producing, your newborn and later, infant is recording some level of that fear, violence and anxiety and so are you.

Consider the feelings you want your baby to record. Limiting television is great, and, if you want to watch something consider the energy of a comedy or moving story. It's important to remember that embryos, newborns, infants and children are absorbing the emotion of what we say or watch. If it elicits a feeling in you, it is exponentially higher in children. No matter how you slice it, television and film are brain programming, sometimes for good, sometimes not.

When my daughter was the age of four, she attended a learning center/daycare. I was unaware, initially that the center showed movies at nap time. Children took turns bringing in a video, many of which have villains and an evil plot line. Suddenly, my daughter, who had never been afraid of the dark or being alone in her room, would have days where she wouldn't go anywhere without me. She wouldn't go outside, go to the bathroom alone or play in another part of our house by herself, saying that she was afraid. She began telling me that the movies at school scared her, and that she didn't want to watch them. After immediate discussion with the teacher, we arranged for my daughter to be in a different class during nap time. I noticed a great improvement at home where she resumed her independence around the house, playing again upstairs while I was downstairs, going in the backyard by herself, etc. It is a long standing thought that children go through a normal stage of development in which they're scared of all kinds of stuff. All children are different, but in mine, I could directly attribute her fear to what had been put in her brain. **Note:** If you are paying for formal daycare, make sure that movies (for the most part) are not watched during this care. You will want to monitor what goes in their brains and … if someone needs a break (time for yourself or the million things you have to do) while your child is watching a movie, it's you.

Media gets stuck in the brain: I have worked with children who have reported scary images repeating in their brain following the viewing of a movie or show or from playing certain video games. In one case, the child had watched a scary news story with his father and became very afraid throughout the day and especially at night. Four weeks later, his mother brought him to see me, saying that her son was having strange scary thoughts. After some digging, we found the cause (the news story) and used brain reprogramming (see last section), to un-stick the scary memory in the brain. Please keep children of all ages from inputting toxic images and concepts because it can become a toxic memory or current thought in the brain. For some children, it is very challenging for them to discern the difference between a thought of theirs verses images they have viewed through media. Thoughts and impulses derived from media are not the essence of your child. Please preserve their essence.

*****I just want to say, "Who thinks putting scary villains, scary scenes and seductive or bitchy female characters into children's films and shows, is good for children?" Apparently, many filmmakers of child films, I guess. This is the time (childhood) when everything is recording, and then going unconscious, possibly resurfacing as an adult fear. Additionally, please be mindful of the programming that can come from princess or other female characters in which young girls begin imitating rude, seductive, entitled or unkind traits, sometimes laced inside well-known films or shows. You know I want to name Disney, but I won't. I met a beautiful, close to six year old girl from India who demonstrated very adult seductive and bossy media driven feminine traits that her parents said came from watching so much Bollywood (film industry in India). What this child would have been will not be known, because her personality has become what she regularly ingested.

*****Connection to the rhythm of nature** is the best way to preserve a child's true rhythm (that they came into the world with).

Monitor, support, and discuss media: Please tell your children very directly when you see them negatively imitating media, that it is not OK. Tell them directly the behavior or trait that is more correctly the best of who your child is, i.e. you are **not** a violent, rude, fire-casting person, you are a strong, kind nearly third grader, using your power for all good things! My daughter is very interested in a character from the Avatar, which is a really awesome series that has great concepts about the earth, energy and so on. Though the series is not something I would have personally exposed my daughter to at age seven, because while there are great concepts, I think the characters act a little too much like teenagers (and my daughter is super absorbent about those kind of things and sometimes already acts/sounds like a teenager ... acculturation, acculturation). Well, I didn't directly share my position on the subject with the Baby Daddy (where my daughter was watching/reading about the Avatar) because of the good messages inside the series and well, as you know, I am particular enough so I try to let some things go. Anyway this female character is very rude and is not necessarily on the good side. But the character is strong, pretty and intriguing, handling her anger with a misuse of her power. Confusing because the character is cool ... but not something a young child can mediate alone. Baby Daddy and I have talked with my daughter about her interest in this slightly evil young woman and about what is OK and not OK, to emulate. However, my daughter was still emulating negative traits of the character, like presenting as a disaffected fifteen year old, casting fire when she is annoyed. So a break was given from watching or reading about the Avatar. Please remind your children continually of their essence and help them to develop their strengths outside of media primarily, and with your guidance! when they are trying on character traits in media.

Search Item: Please check out Common Sense Media, www.commonsensemedia.org which provides reviews, age ratings and other information about kid movies and all types of media.

Strengthen creative play: As a parent, I know some days are long and frankly your child watching movies or otherwise are the breaks you need or the momentary babysitter. I get it. I have done it, many times. I also know that when my child watches too much, it is not that much different from the sugar addiction that I describe in the nutrition section of the book. My daughter becomes whiny, only wants more, complains of being bored and temporarily forgets about that great imaginary play that really creates the brain connections I want her to have. When she watches short term clips, or none at all, that behavior is much less or nonexistent.

14. CHLORINE:

Chlorine also needs to be considered if you are drinking tap water, and bathing your children. At this point, I know you're thinking, "Oh my gosh, I have to put my baby in a plastic bubble, but oh gosh, I can't use the plastic!" (This reminds me ... please research BPA free, plastic drinking vessels for your baby.) Just remember, take the information, then do the best you can. OK, back to it! I recommend drinking spring water or filtered water through your pregnancy, and beyond. Check out local springs in your area, where you can fill up your glass bottles, for free. Also, consider buying a filter for your shower, and/or doing cloth washes, and less daily baths for children, under the age of five or buying a house with well water. **Note:** There are other issues with tap water besides chlorine, including fluoride (see dental section), along with run off issues from sewage. Please research.

SPECIAL NOTE: Please Google the Centers for Disease Control (CDC) about chlorine. It says that chlorine was used during World War I as a choking agent. It also says that chlorine is also currently used in some pesticides and water treatment. So ... if your child is having lung issues please consider the water (drinking, bathing, swimming) and please consider the foods that have been sprayed with pesticides.

Yeah, so, whenever possible, only swim in natural bodies of water during pregnancy, such as lakes or oceans and please purchase foods free of pesticides. Please keep this in mind as your child grows. By products of chlorine have been found in the urine of swimmers thirty minutes after swimming (http://jonbarron.org/article/danger-swimming-chlorinated-pools#.VH4plmd0yM8b, 2011). In young children, absorption of chemicals occurs much more intensely than it does for adults, because of the blood-brain barrier deal. One of chlorine's byproducts is haloacetic acid (HAAs), a dangerous chemical allowed in restricted amounts in our drinking water by the Environmental Protection Agency. HAA is associated with cancer and birth defects (http://jonbarron.org/article/danger-swimming-chlorinated-pools#.VH4plmd0yM8b, 2011). One of my clients reported that her one-year old daughter would not sleep well, sometimes for days, after playing in chlorinated water.

My daughter and I moved around a bit in her early years. We lived by a river, which we swam in, and then we lived by the ocean, which we also happily swam in. Now we live by a lake, which we happily swim in. However my daughter's paternal grandparents have a pool ... and of course, my daughter, like her mama loves being in water and having fun. Who doesn't? I do know families who will not swim in chlorine at all. If I had known information about chlorine as thoroughly as I do now, I might have adopted the no chlorine swim. I do try to avoid it, but it's not always easy. Maybe more people will just start converting their chlorine pools to salt water pools, which would be amazing!

I would like to say that more and more families are educating themselves about choices that affect the health of their children. However, you may be around families who are not yet making these kinds of choices. Be strong, one family doing it differently is how twenty families are given information. Some may initially reject it, but most will be curious. When you tell them why you don't swim in chlorine, or why you are making other more natural choices, they will learn something important, and likely, change something in their child's life. This is how we make a difference!

Search Item: Effects of chlorine on infants and children.

15. DIAPERS:

Using cloth diapers is not as hard as it might seem. Soft cloth on the bottom is more comfortable, as opposed to the make-up of traditional diapers. It's easy to throw them in a covered bin and then into the wash. Babies who use cloth diapers become more aware of their bodies because they can feel when their diaper is wet, immediately. This body awareness, possibly makes potty training easier down the road, with hopefully fewer accidents once trained. See http://homeguides.sfgate.com/benefits-cloth-diapers-78695.html, for more info.

Another powerful way to create connection to the body, is through elimination communication (EC), which involves using a very tiny potty and recognizing signals that your infant has to urinate or otherwise. Newborns can do this. You become so much more tuned to their body, and therefore, they stay tuned to theirs. It's pretty amazing and really keeps you connected to your baby at a deeper level. My five month old was delighted to sit on the potty (with sometimes pillows on either side of her), and, when I was at home, I would sometimes get up to five eliminations in that day. Please, please research. **Note:** My sister Jennifer began EC with her third child day one, baby born and peeing on the potty! We started EC (not consistently) when my daughter was about one month old and began using it more frequently when she was around four months old. When she could crawl off the potty at eight or nine months old, it was more challenging to stick with it. But, there are people out there who EC and really don't use diapers at all. It could be you!

If you need to supplement your cloth diaper system or really know you are a disposable diaper family, please use natural diapers, found at Whole Foods, sometimes at Target or purchased online. Please use natural wipes as well, which can be found at Job Lot for less than three dollars. Babies can have sensitivities that show up as frequent diaper rashes, due to the chemicals (like possibly chlorine) found in typical diapers. (**Side note:** Diapers biodegrading on the earth with chemicals in it … not good for anyone.) Chlorine absorbs through the skin. It is also inhaled, which means chlorine is passing freely through the brain of infants, because of their underdeveloped blood-brain barrier. It means that chlorine is possibly mingling with brain development, and affecting genetic expression. Please research.

My daughter on EC potty … 4.5 months old.

16. SOAPS/CLEANERS:

So as you know, my friends think I'm a bit of a freak, but they love me just the same. I tell them that I will practically faint or begin speaking in tongues if they spray their blue ammonia near me. Bleach makes me immediately feel like I've had a sinus infection for six months and unnatural soaps and shampoos cause severe vomiting (this is a joke, but I really do get bloody noses from bleach). Anyway, I am super sensitive and would like to now admit to everyone, that because I keep my system so pure, I can perceive toxins. I don't usually say this out loud because I would sound like a total A-hole and it would be akin to saying "my poop literally smells like roses."

With that said, please use natural (organic whenever possible) lotions, soaps and shampoos. Even soaps, lotions, etc., that say natural, can have toxic chemicals, so please, read labels. Sixty to seventy percent of what we apply to the skin is absorbed into the body. Consideration should be given to your infant, but especially, for yourself while pregnant and really don't forget you, with baby in or out of you. You are important too! Sodium Lauryl Sulfate and its close relative Sodium Laureth Sulfate (SLES) are commonly used in shampoos, soaps, toothpastes and more. Please research this. It's linked to neurological issues, skin problems and cancer (http://www.natural-health-information-centre.com/sodium-lauryl-sulfate.html#ixzz3KmMTqUNN).

*****Super please check out the effects of <u>parabens</u>, also in almost all shampoos and hygiene products, particularly deodorants. It's highly linked to breast cancer. Please keep this in mind when you are pregnant, and especially while nursing. If parabens are found in breasts with breast cancer (please research ... articles available at mercola.com) we don't want babies drinking parabens in their breast milk. Embryos and infants bathed in these sorts of chemicals will have no choice but to adapt normal cell growth to the compounds of these unnatural agents, thereby making an individual possibly susceptible to unhealthy genetic expression.

Inhaling chemicals is another consideration for the same reasons. A shift to natural cleaners is important, as well. Trader Joe's has very well priced cleaners, dish/laundry soap, soap and shampoos. Many of these products have similar ingredients, so if you run out of one, you can substitute another. I have made their dish soap into hand soap and used my shampoo to clean toilets and scrub showers. The large 365 laundry detergent from Whole Foods, for ten or so dollars, can be used in the dish washer and also successfully scrubs toilets, sinks and showers. Economics and air quality can work together. **Note:** If you have a professional cleaning person come to your home, consider giving them natural cleaners to replace the super toxic fumes from bleach and other products. Please research how these chemicals can be an underlying cause of skin, lung and stomach issues. Though your child may not have a visible symptom, these types of cleaners, particularly bleach, may cause duress on the system. If you have pets, they will also benefit from your shift away from these toxins.

Tip: Add large house plants for cleaner air and a more serene environment. Large house plants are easier to take care of then smaller ones and provide a stronger air purification system. Be sure to research plants that are safe for young children.

17. CLOTHING/BEDDING:

I often worked on this book in the early, early morning, sometimes 4:30 am. When my daughter awoke, she'd creep downstairs, curl up into my arms and ask what I was working on. One day, I read her the table of contents. She said, "Did you tell them (the mommies) to buy organic clothes?" She said that if the babies don't wear organic clothes, "the chemicals will get on the babies' skin, and they (the babies) will cry, and the mommies won't know why" and so, I added this category. When it comes to newborns, I believe the sensitivity to chemicals in fabric can absolutely, be that high. Not just newborns, but infants and young children are rapidly absorbing unwanted chemicals as well. Remember, chemicals can change the biology and influence the expression of DNA, in a not so good way (www.motherjones.com/blue-marble/2012/06/can-exposure-toxins-change-your-dna). If you want more of a National Institute of Health, pub med type article, there are plenty to this regard.

For most of my daughter's life, we have functioned at, or just above poverty level income (things have improved greatly since beginning my private practice two or so years ago). We made our way through with luck, hand-me-downs and a prayer. I always bought organic food, with creativity and lots of potatoes. Organic clothing purchases did not make the budget, but I was grateful for the gifts from other mothers and families, ready to pass on what they had finished with. Recycling clothes is a great way to help the planet and so we passed on our clothes as well.

However, if you have the means and are going to purchase new towels, bedding and clothing, really consider buying all organic. You will be giving your child less toxins absorbed through the skin and less toxins in their general air quality. If a six year old (at the time) intuits that babies cry because of the chemicals in clothing, it's truly worth looking into. Lastly, the extra dollars you spend on organic clothing and bedding can be considered an important environmental contribution to organic farmers, organic businesses, and therefore, the earth as a whole. What a wonderful way to begin a life, with an intention to be part of something larger that really, really matters.

*****Every single choice we make means something, it either gives or it takes, and what we give is given back to us in health, love and beauty.* **Side note:** I think the bolded italicized sentence that I just wrote sounds poetic and lovely, I could even be a little proud of myself. But the truth is, I just went to Stop & Shop and bought toilet paper not made of recycled materials only because they didn't have any toilet paper made from recycled materials. (Stop & Shop please carry only recycled paper products and paper product makers please use only recycled materials.) Still, I could have stopped at another store. I guess what I'm saying is, I'm a person who likes her modern conveniences and I am sure you do too. We just have to do the best we can. If we make five really green choices out of seven, well then the earth wins, not pollution or corporations who drown butterflies. You know I still love you corporations but I might have to call you up and yell "stupid mofo jackass" if you dump any more chemicals into rivers, streams, lakes or oceans. I am sure once the anger is released and your dazed confusion about being separate from the grounds/waters you pollute … cleared, we will launch into great ideas that really surprise people. You know you are a really good listener, I'm so glad we're friends.

Oh, if you forgot the topic because of the side note that went on a bit of a tangent, please purchase organic clothing, bedding and so on, if you have the means.

Search Items: Organic clothing, mattresses, bedding. Infant sensitivity to chemicals in fabric.

18. NUTRITION/SUPPLIMENTS:

Baby Food: Breast milk forever! Then if you have to feed your child something … go organic and make it yourself, if you can. Avocado/olive oil and sea salt is the perfect baby food and is great for brain development, beginning at four months or later. Sweet potato cooked and mashed, olive oil and sea salt is another great one. Babies can gnaw on raw carrots for vitamins and minerals, and to assist with teething (always supervise babies gnawing on carrots please). Coconut products are superfoods, so consider adding coconut oil to anything and everything you can, use coconut milk and coconut yogurt. Though coconut milk has some of the same good-for-you fatty acids found in mama's milk, remember always, the number one baby food is your breast milk. If you don't want to make your own food, consider brands like Plum Organics that have this sort of labeling:

Always certified organic
Unsweetened, unsalted, and no artificial ingredients
Non-GMO Project Verified
BPA-free packaging & child safe, recyclable cap

Search Items: www.wisegeek.com*/what-are-the-***benefits-***of-***coconut-oil-for-babies** and
wholesomebabyfood.momtastic.com */organicsfor***homemadebabyfood.***htm*

Gluten and Dairy: Consider a gluten and dairy free diet for your child until the age of five or six, and potentially longer. Newborns, infants and young children have very sensitive systems of digestion. Gluten affects the intestines, which affects the brain and other functions of the body, linked to all kinds of physical issues (please research), and down the road, possibly behavioral /emotional issues as well www.drkaslowglutenbrain connection.htm.

Dairy can have the same effects. A wonderful mother shared her painful story of her daughter who cried for the first three months of life. Initially, the infant was thought to be colic. The family later discovered that their daughter had a significant dairy allergy. The mother learned that the molecules of cow's milk are much too large to pass through the intestinal system of infants, causing pain for some. When the family went dairy free, her daughter stopped crying endlessly. Maybe, colic has been a dairy allergy all along.

When gluten and dairy are removed from the diet, some families report the resolution of issues such as eczema, chronic coughs, crankiness/irritability, as well as toddler behavior problems (beyond normal toddler behavior) and ADD/ADHD. One mother reported that when gluten was removed from their diet, it was a miracle for their household. They felt completely overrun and controlled by the behavior of their overly inflexible toddler. Within 24 hours, the family had a more congenial and flexible child. In addition, the diet change resolved a leaky urine and bowel issue for their three year old. It's important to note that eliminating foods such as gluten and dairy from the diet can cause worsening behaviors or symptoms due to withdrawal in the system. Consult with a naturopath. For some families, improvements take a week to a month or even longer. Hang in there, it's worth it.

Though I did not have much gluten or dairy in my daughter's diet, we had some. A functional medicine doctor told me that the black circles around my (at the time) three year old daughter's eyes and runny nose was likely due to an intolerance for gluten and dairy. He explained that intestines are connected to the sinuses, so difficulty digesting these clogging foods could be the culprit. When we removed gluten and dairy from her diet, the runny nose cleared up completely AND my intense toddler became so much more flexible!!! AND her impulse to chew on things stopped! It was life changing! When my now seven year old daughter ingests gluten or dairy (which is super rare), she sometimes displays that impulse to chew on things and seems a little edgy, so we stay away from it as much as possible. I admit to being a sucker for a few important dairy items such as raw cheese on special occasions, cream in my coffee when I forgot to bring my own almond milk and maybe one or two other rare or low dairy value items. My daughter endures a stricter plan, at least for now, although a gluten-free cheese pizza gets in there on occasion.

A few other thoughts on this...

*****I think that no gluten and dairy for pregnant and nursing mothers could be lumped into other food caution categories, such as no tuna fish or blue cheese. There are lots and lots of alternatives now, including gluten-free cakes, cookies and breads. The alternatives to cow's milk are delicious, such as almond, hemp, rice and coconut milk. Daiya makes a great nondairy cheese.

*****As said above, Gluten and dairy greatly affect the gut. A pregnant mother's intestinal bacteria affects the brain development of the fetus, specifically, the development of the blood-brain barrier. Check out the article titled *Mother's Microbes affects Baby's Brain's* (2014) www.thescientist, article number 41476.

*****Before you allow a teacher or other professional to recommend medication for your child's inability to focus or, for hyperactivity, please consider taking them off gluten and dairy (please consult with a naturopath). I truly believe we can get away from giving young children stimulants that predispose them to addiction issues or lifelong prescription drug dependence by changing their diets.

***** Please research gluten and dairy-free recipes online. There are so many great ones out there!!! Here's one for superfood French toast ... gluten-free bread, hemp milk, coconut oil and cinnamon. Maple syrup or, if your child is older than one, you can spread raw honey over the toast.

*****I could go on about gluten and dairy-free (because I think it so important!), but we still have so much to talk about. I trust you will find what you need to know.

No GMOs: Please stay away from genetically modified foods (GMOs) (please research) which like wheat, can have the unwanted effects of turning on genetics that you don't want, and silencing the ones you do. Look for labels that say Non-GMO verified ... particularly when it comes to canola oil!, corn, soy, wheat and potato.

Sugar: Please, please do not create a sugar-addicted baby and child. Seriously, make your life easier and your child's. When you give your child refined sugar at a young age, it literally carves pathways in the brain. These pathways will want to support themselves with more sugar. It creates a monster in the grocery store when the child cries and tantrums until you're forced to provide their addiction with more sugar. If you don't give them sugar, they will not crave it. For my daughter, she understood by age two, that when we went to birthday parties or other occasions where they served sugary foods, we would eat an alternative yummy snack, such as gluten-free/dairy free cookies sweetened with maple syrup or honey, and coconut ice cream sweetened with agave. Because she's growing up this way, she is clear both physically and emotionally about the issue (most of the time). She understands that putting sugar in your body creates problems. This body awareness is strengthening in children and can assist in empowering lifelong wellness.

***** I think children who have a different diet from their peers get the added benefit of learning refusal skills and delayed gratification, which is certainly linked to stronger teenagers and more successful adults.

Sugar is linked to children with attention/hyperactivity problems and obesity. I believe sugar moves astrocytes out of their resting "all is well" place, possibly making an environment more favorable for junk/unhealthy genetics to be expressed. Additionally, I think glial cells will make pathways based on the short-term high derived from sugar and will seek to support the neuro-structure by eating more sugar, not unlike the pathways and behavior of a drug addict (and in the meantime, making children quite hyper). Further, glial cells are tripped into communicating a need for sugar (instead of glial cells being used for creativity and learning), possibly forming pathways for obesity, an epidemic in our country.

*****I really love people and understand … but when I hear about kids getting real doughnuts (there are gluten-free healthy-ish ones) or going to the ice cream man, I think it's like how I feel about racism, "is this really still happening?" Seriously, you **must** think a man driving a truck selling gross, sugar addicting red-dye dripping down the face food, is creepy. It's so creepy. When I hear that bell, I feel like I am in a 1980s horror movie with clowns who do bad things. Please, somebody make a line of earth trucks which educate children about health, selling coconut ice cream, raw chocolates and maple gluten-free cookies. Please hire women and men who don't play a ton of video games in their spare time … yes, strange random thought. Speaking of video games, you could imagine that I am not a fan of overusing them, especially violent ones. Astrocytes programmed and programmed and programmed. Adrenaline and cortisol elevation messages sent and sent and sent. This is easily linked to anxiety and other issues. It doesn't mean I am against all video games and that my daughter hasn't come across them or ever played them or that I sometimes go the gas station for Green Mountain coffee and put real cow cream in it, even when I don't know how the cows were treated. Somehow video games snuck into the sugar addiction category as did my coffee habits. Hmm. **Note:** It is very important to know that I have very close friends who occasionally feed their children frosting in spoonfuls, friends who consider eating guinea pigs a delicacy and friends with an interest in taxidermy. When I say no judgment I mean it. You will still find dozens of hypocrisies in my life. Please be gentle with me when you find them, I will change if you ask me. *****We have to at least talk about the ideal and then do the best we can without comparing or judging! I totally love you!

Search Item: The effects of sugar on the child brain.

Food has a DNA code: Avoid microwaving food. All life has a DNA code, microwaving can change the structure of that code with high heat and rapid sound waves. I theorize that the food's altered structure can possibly interrupt glial cell function on a small level. *Do the best you can with this, I admit to using the microwave when I have no other options, like when I'm at Whole Foods and my daughter wants a gluten-free bagel (immediately!) from the freezer section. I microwave for 10 seconds or so, just so I can cut it, then I toast it. Oh and sometimes, I have used the microwave for my own lunch at work (rarely) and in the first grade I stole flash cards from the teacher. Yup! ... put them right in my bag, at a Catholic School. I did feel really guilty and returned them (without the teacher knowing or ever owning up).

Meat: None.

Meat: I'm kidding ... half kidding. OK please buy organic meat from really nice farmers who worked with Temple Grandin. She taught farmers to use white sheets to guide their cows to slaughter, so the cows don't feel terrifying fear. Pesticide adrenaline meat from a cow who lived life like they were at a concentration camp, cannot be good for anyone, especially the cow. Please think about how the cow was cared for when ingesting dairy as well. No hormone milk. Don't forget the pigs ... who may spend their lives in small cages, and piglets whose lives are cut short for a higher-end ham and bacon. Please research who you are buying from. If you cannot afford organic well-treated animals, then please eat beans.

Chicken/Eggs/Fish: None

Chicken/Eggs/Fish: Oh there I go again with radical kidding. Please buy organic chicken, who have lived a descent life and could go anywhere they wanted to go (free range). So when the chicken is on your plate you taste respect and freedom, not factory anxiety. Fish and mercury ... please research. Teach your children to thank the chicken or fish or eggs and cow too! The chickens feel extreme pressure and work very hard to produce eggs at rates well beyond normal (Thank you Jeanette Dias for that spark of information). Don't get me wrong, I have sat at diners, sipping on coffee, the morning post New Year's Eve party, not thinking twice about ordering a three egg omelet. It is just that if the earth is going to be OK, we can't live like a mid-evil king with a drumstick in our mouth thinking that the peasant (the cow or chicken in this case) is in love with serving us. The peasant is suffering and if you eat suffering, well, then you suffer. I don't want you to, and believe me I sometimes want to live like there is no tomorrow too (and sometimes do, sorry ... getting better every day). Maybe we'll go to a small, local, super Zen farmer, buy some organic eggs and make a really nice brunch at our house with soy candles, good music ... it's not a sacrifice. It is more beautiful than we thought.

Vegetarian Protein: Organic beans, bean pasta, lentils, quinoa, nuts, seeds, tempeh and gluten-free Quorn products made of mushroom-like protein.

Fruits and Veggies: Organic lots of them ... preferably picked in your backyard or locally.

Grains: Organic everything. Brown rice, gluten-free buckwheat, oats and granola, millet, amaranth, quinoa. Limit or stay away from corn products when possible.

*****The above is just a short skinny on food. Please research recipes and high nutrition for you and your child. Oh, this is just a random thought, please don't forget about supplemental probiotics (for the gut) or eat a ton of pickles (fermented foods are very good probiotics). As said earlier, please research gut health, it is so super important for you while pregnant, nursing and for your children as they grow.

Essential oils for best health of infant and child: Essential oils are truly essential supplements for children (I believe), because they are the most concentrated part of the plant, and the plant's immune system. Lavender or chamomile can aid in a calm disposition, relieve allergies or assist in deeper sleep. Some oils require an oil base, such as jojoba, grape seed or olive oil before direct skin application. As said earlier, if you are choosing not to immunize you might be especially interested in researching oils such as cinnamon and sage (which require an oil base before applying). They have high anti-microbial and anti-viral properties. Thieves stealing from the dead bodies of those afflicted with the plague, used essential oils to protect themselves from becoming diseased. It is powerful stuff.

When my daughter was born at home, we used a humidifier, regularly adding red thyme, so that this highly anti-bacterial, anti-microbial, anti-viral oil would create clean air for our new baby. (*Note red thyme cannot be applied directly to the skin, because it is so strong.) Coconut oil rubbed directly on the baby's body is also another highly anti-bacterial, anti-viral agent, and with essential oils added to this base, you have a power house of health assurance.

The following is a list obtained from Young Living's Product Information. Young Living is a company that sells high grade essential oil. It's convenient to grab essential oils at Whole Foods or another natural food store, though you can probably get higher grade oils online. Please research and/or consult with an aromatherapist.

*****Please note that many of the oils below can be applied (after being mixed in a base oil) to you, the mother, which will come through to your child, via breast milk. I know I am repeating myself ... but, it is very important to research oils that are safe for babies, children and breastfeeding mothers.

Allergies: eucalyptus, lavender
Antibiotics: clove, oregano, lemon, cinnamon, eucalyptus
Antiseptic: eucalyptus, lemon, cinnamon, clove
Aches in Bones: lemongrass, peppermint, vetiver, basil
ADD/ADHD: lavender, basil, frankincense, vetiver
Burns/Cuts: lavender, peppermint, clove, lemongrass
Colds/Flu: lemon, eucalyptus, peppermint
Digestion: peppermint
Depression: bergamot, ylang ylang, sage, lavender
Headaches: lavender, sage, ylang ylang

Sleep Issues: lavender
Nausea: peppermint, lavender
Respiratory: eucalyptus, bergamot, basil
Skin: frankincense, lavender, ylang ylang

*****Please look into essential oils as bug and tick repellants. I have used citronella and white thyme oil rubbed on ankles, hats and the back of the neck (test first please). Your kids won't like the smell, but neither do ticks. Peppermint and eucalyptus are other good ones.

Home Remedies: Don't be afraid to find the solution yourself, when your child is not feeling well (of course, serious issues require a doctor's attention). When my daughter had a fever, a friend told me to eat a ton of raw garlic so that my breast milk could knock out the problem (it always did). When my daughter was three, she woke in the middle of the night with an earache, so I quickly looked online and found that vinegar distilled in water (or urine from you or a pagan high priestess), poured directly into the ear could fix the issue, and it did. I chose the vinegar, not the urine. Chamomile and olive oil rubbed on the gums is great for teething; coconut oil, rubbed all over your child's body, brings down a fever, and eucalyptus rubbed on the chest is great for coughs.

Speaking wellness: By age three, I taught my daughter that her body will listen to what she says, and to tell it to be well. Even when she's been cuddled up in bed with a fever and cold, we would say together, "I am healthy. I am healthy. I am healthy." Additionally, when my daughter sleeps, I speak to those brain cells, the glial cells, saying things like, "You are wonderful, healthy and of perfect well-being." It's very, very important not to convey any worry about your child's health in emotion (if possible), and not in conversation in front of them, even newborns and infants. Those glial cells are recording, recording, recording and then sending messages onto the body. Keep things optimistic. Tell the body what you want for health, it will listen. **Note:** I am kind of the "no complaint" Nazi in my house and my daughter will likely go through a rebellious period in her teenager years of rampant complaining. Then she will go off to college, get a horrible cold that won't go away right before a happening party that she wants to attend, call me, and say, "Mom, can we do that thing, where we talk to my cells and make the illness go away." I will not respond with hurt from the burning teenage years, but will say, "I love you, of course, sweetie."

Consult with a naturopath: Consulting with a naturopath can be a very helpful way to get started on the home remedy path. Their understanding of the interaction between herbs, homeopathy and supplements with the body is very, very valuable in making major changes in how your child feels physically, and also, changes in their behavior. For example, you might make an appointment for issues such as sleep problems, eczema, asthma, tantrums that seem beyond typical, allergies, dietary concerns, child behavior problems and tongue ties.

Breast milk remedies: Breastfeeding prevents many illnesses from becoming more serious or, from occurring at all. Beyond ingesting it, breast milk can be poured into a baby's ear when they're tugging on it or crying due to pain from it. Breast milk can also be applied directly to cuts and scrapes, as a natural antiseptic. Please research.

A recipe to make well: Blended apple juice, cinnamon, garlic, Camu Camu and Bentonite clay for breastfeeding mama. Skip the garlic if you are giving the drink directly to your child, otherwise they will likely spit it out all over your best dress. Why you are wearing your best dress while you are attending your sick child is not for me to judge. All of these items can be found at Whole Foods.

Tip: In my experience, the employees in the supplement department at Whole Foods are great and have a lot of information. You can say, "I need a natural antibiotic." They might say "OK, you can try colloidal silver, golden seal or cats claw." It's amazing! Don't be afraid to ask about health issues that don't require a doctor's attention (when you do go to the doctor, hopefully they have both holistic and traditional information).

*****We all know that hand washing is super important. Well, my daughter has had two warts on her fingers. Dear friend and APRN Nicole Casbarro told me to use apple cider vinegar and a band aid daily until they fell off. The whole daily band aid thing was not working for us. So I created an apple cider vinegar, water and essential oil white thyme hand wash. In just over two weeks of this, one wart has already come off, and the other is on its way. Nature always has a solution, trust it! This hand wash remedy could be a good alternative to antibacterial soaps (which I use in public places) that could disrupt your good bacteria (please research).

Backyard garden: Consider having a backyard garden. What you organically grow has such a high level of nutrition, and the greatest living value in your system (unless you are drinking breast milk), because you are picking off the stem. The food hasn't traveled in boxes across the country handled by people and systems (though I primarily have gotten my food this way, up until 10 or so months ago, when I moved to an apartment with a very large organic garden). A garden in your backyard means you can visit it, every morning, putting little bare feet in the dirt to investigate what's grown. You can share vegetables with neighbors, make pickles together and of course, most importantly, eat vibrant food planted by your hands, and your child's little hands. These kinds of activities stick firmly in a child's memory, because of the grounded nature of the task, and the quality of the food is like medicine.

Visiting a Pediatrician: I would like to introduce a very, very dear friend, Dr. Diana Lopusny of Preferred Pediatrics, a vibrant and courageous pediatrician in Milford, CT. She started her practice seven years ago and has become one of the few, if not only pediatrician's office within one hundred miles, who offers both traditional and holistic medicine. In my opinion, she is a forerunner in the treatment of children and I hope that pediatricians will model their care from her expertise. Not only is she a brilliant woman, she is funny, loving and exuberant and every one of her patients receives this life in her care. I have been extremely fortunate to operate my private practice inside her office.

SPECIAL SIDE NOTE: In 2013, I up and moved to Milford, CT to a cute little cottage close to the beach. I was working with Yale Prevention Research Center at the time fine tuning a research protocol that I developed using the brain programming treatment (detailed in later sections). I ardently hoped that we would receive a grant and I would work there full-time. Milford is close to Derby (where Yale Prevention Research Center is). Milford has a Whole Foods, Trader Joes and a Montessori School ... I thought "this is perfect!" Life does not always make turns for the reason you think, but it makes turns. I made plans to work at a naturopath's office in the meantime, until a grant came through and so I moved. All set in a beautiful little cottage and the naturopath office falls through. So… on a desperate day, I said to my then four year old, "Honey, please go put a dress on, Mommy needs a job." I walked into Rainbow Gardens a really dear-to-me restaurant in Milford, where I was hired on that desperate day with my four year old in tow. For that summer (which turned into a whole year), I waitressed with wonderful staff and owners, who treated me like family. I am forever grateful. (Coincidently the Rainbow Gardens' owner keeps bees on the roof of their restaurant, donates their fry oil for reuse, uses recycled paper products and buys local and organic whenever possible. They also let me bring my daughter to work, when I had no one to watch her.) Anyway, sometime in late 2013, I called up Dr. Lopusny and asked her if I could have a private practice in her office, which HAPPENED to be five minutes from that little beach cottage. Dr. Lopusny said she had been wanting, the right therapist for her office … the stable, eccentric, holistic type who can appreciate Italian hand gestures and office hugs … "Well, then I am your girl" or politically correct woman! So … by listening to the leap to move to Milford, I was not only given time in that waitressing/beach life for research (my daughter would play on the beach and I would pour through research articles), I was given an office (said again for drama) FIVE minutes from my home in one of the only holistic pediatrician offices in the state. When life (divine force to some) turns, let it turn you, try not to go kicking, crying and screaming like I sometimes do.

Holistic/traditional blend of medicine: Dr. Lopusny has given us a few examples of how she might blend holistic and traditional medicine with patients that present with certain symptoms. Obviously, if you need to see a doctor, please do! Like the rest of the book, this segment is meant to give you a spark of information, it is not meant to diagnose or treat.

For example, in a typical Pediatricians office **coughing/colds** might be recommended an over the counter cough syrup, or possibly an antibiotic, depending on the severity. In Dr. Lopusny's office, a family could be advised to do a series of hot showers, while taking honey, herbals or may receive a referral to a homeopath. For **asthma**, the recommendation could be a nebulizer and immune boosters to decrease inflammation, such as fish oil and vitamin A. For **eczema**, a child is typically treated with steroids. In Dr. Lopusny's practice, their team would attempt to get to the source of the issue by finding out what foods might be aggravating the gut or looking into biological/environmental concerns that could be related. The eczema would be treated topically with coconut oil as the first intervention.

For **toddler tantrums** and other child behavior issues such as **ADHD**, Dr. Lopusny and her team typically look first at nutrition and diet with recommendations to remove inflammatory foods such as gluten, dairy, soy and corn (with dairy and gluten being the most important). A consult with a homeopath is also advised. Herbals such as skull cap or use of Rescue Remedy can be helpful for child tantrums. Consider research on chiropractic adjustments and its effects on the spine and behavior, said Dr. Lopusny. She gasps at medication as the first line for children diagnosed with ADHD, particularly since miracles happen in these cases just by changing the diet (particularly no gluten and no dairy.) Blood work and genetic testing are also recommended by Dr. Lopusny in childhood diagnoses such as ADHD.

Dr. Lopusny said that **sleep issues** can be worked through with adjustments to the sleep environment, working with a gentle sleep specialist, homeopathy, chamomile and possibly co-sleeping. **Fevers** are typically prescribed aspirin or Motrin, which Dr. Lopusny says, their team reserves for extreme situations. She states that fevers can be good and can assist the body to fight infection. Wet socks on the feet help congestion and fevers. Homeopathic belladonna is helpful in a fever situation and Dr. Lopusny states that a chiropractic adjustment almost always breaks a fever.

For **viral and bacterial infections**, immune boosters are the key, says Dr. Lopusny. Though she says there are cases where an antibiotic is necessary such as with strep, pneumonia and urinary tract infections. Dr. Lopusny said there are many immune boosters and named Echinacea, elderberry, high doses of vitamin C and D, teas with honey, rose hips tea especially, and ginger, garlic and turmeric in juicing. Dr. Lopusny stated that patients with the flu are typically prescribed Tamiflu. She said there are other options such as Oscillococcicum or Triple Flu Defense by Dr. Nenninger. She further recommends tons of immune support for the flu and, in many child illnesses, immune support is the key. Thank you again Dr. Lopusny!

19. DENTAL HEALTH:

After your pediatrician fires you (hopefully not), next comes your dentist when you tell them no fluoride treatments please (if you want to). I recently told my new dentist this, who gave me the lecture about the importance of fluoride and then still took me in. After the lecture, he then said, "I will tell you" sort of secretly, with his eyes a little squinty and dark, that his wife refused to allow their children fluoride treatments or fluoride toothpaste and he said ... their children, now teenagers, have no cavities. "Oh damn," I said to myself, "the cat is out the dental black bag ... the teeth can stay strong without fluoride." (By the way, this dentist is really one of the most gentle, open and awesome dentists I have come across. I hope you find a cool one too!)

Pineal gland and fluoride: Please go to the National Institute of Health. Then go to the search bar and type in pineal gland and fluoride. Up comes research articles on said topic. Then go back up to the section of the book on the pineal gland, remembering how important this gland is!

Research shows fluoride affects the brain: Dear FDA: please consider the following that was retrieved from http//fluoridealert.org/studies/brain01/:

> As of November 2015, a total of 56 studies have investigated the relationship between fluoride and human intelligence, and a total of 36 studies have investigated the relationship between fluoride and learning/memory in animals (again sorry to the animals and thank you for your contribution, may it be of high value). Of these investigations, 49 of the 56 human studies have found that elevated fluoride exposure is associated with reduced IQ, while 34 of the 36 animal studies have found that fluoride exposure impairs the learning and/or memory capacity of animals. The human studies, which are based on IQ examinations of over 12,000 children, provide compelling evidence that fluoride exposure during the early years of life can damage a child's brain.

Fluoride Alert has all kinds of articles and information such as fluoride's effect on the fetal brain, fluoride's calcifying effect on the bones and pineal gland, and further states that *97 % of Western Europe has rejected water fluoridation.* I think it is important to note that this site mentions that fluoride is not a nutrient ... it is medicine and that there should be choice in choosing medicine in drinking water. **Note:** Some public schools are still giving children weekly cups of liquid neurotoxins (fluoride), and the Nazis gave their captives fluoride to weaken their resistance, so did the Russians. (It is not that I think that loving public schools are trying to weaken their children, it is that loving public schools have been told that they are helping children, in the same way, loving dentists are taught.)

*****__Please look into how fluoride affects iodine absorption and the thyroid. Maybe such high rates of obesity (iodine/thyroid issue) in America have something to do with fluoride in our waters.__ Not sure, but worth a look. It would be nice if it were somehow easier for people and children to think well and feel well in their bodies. Not thinking well and not feeling well has become an epidemic in people and children. We can make a difference by researching and informing each other.

Kate Gorman's holistic dental program: (Keep in mind I am not a dentist, I am a mother, who is **Gut + Research**ing it, like you.)

1.) Teeth brushing two to three times a day with no fluoride toothpaste. There are several brands available online, in Whole Foods and in other natural food stores. Earth Paste and Dessert Essence are great brands. Please no sodium lauryl sulfate in your toothpaste either. Please do the brushing for your children until at least age seven, unless you have three or four children, then just get the youngest ones and have everybody brush together, timed for at least two minutes.

2.) Rinse mouth with coconut oil at least three times per week, for five minutes at a time, beginning at age 3 or age 4. If you can add turmeric into your coconut oil, without your child throwing up, even better! (Turmeric, baking soda and coconut oil, great teeth whitener.) I didn't begin this, coconut oil swishing, until my daughter was age 7 and I am not always on top of it, to be honest. I want to be! Another thing I am not great at (for my daughter) is flossing. Again, I aspire to be and you certainly can do it, I know you can!

3.) Provide mineralizing supplements such as a small amount of maca root in a nondairy milks like coconut or almond. Purchase chlorella tablets for children to chew on, great for teeth, brain development and more! Please research other mineralizing supplements and herbal teas, such as oat straw and horsetail. Salt is also mineralizing. Sea salt is great, but iodine salt is super important for teeth and other processes. Please research.

4.) Avoid processed sugar, but also excessive amounts of dried fruit and fruit juices. We have such a simple diet, that I have included lots of dried mangos, frozen blueberries, apple juice and so on. But, at age 7, my daughter has had two small teeth sealants. Not a big deal, but something I need to work on as far as cleaning the teeth directly following consumption of such fruit products or changing the type of snack at school when I can't clean her teeth directly after.

5.) Please see a super cool dentist for regular cleanings (without fluoride).

6.) Please do not use mercury fillings!!!

7.) Please consider healthy gum, such as gum with Xylitol in it, which when used throughout the day may reduce tooth decay and overall oral health (that's what it says on the Xylitol gum packages). Again, this is found in Whole Foods and other natural health stores. Please consider the level of monitoring needed relative to your child's age, when providing gum (I say this because I sort of think I'm supposed to, not because I think you're not gonna watch your kid. I think you're rockin' awesome and your kid is going to change the world, with hopefully a smile and mouth full of beautiful teeth!). Please also avoid gum with sugar or artificial sweeteners in it.

SPECIAL NOTE: <u>Dear FDA, please consider Xylitol for its remineralizing effects on teeth and as a possible alternative to fluoride</u> (Yanangisawa, T., Miake Y. Saeki, Y. and Takahashi, M., 2003).

*****Please research other natural protocols, supplements and holistic dentists. This is an area where I need more research myself. We can do it together!

20. MOLD/AIR TOXINS:

I am really not trying to make you a paranoid, type A, anal, helicopter parent, but air toxins and mold inhalation can also affect a baby/child's health, particularly their skin and lungs. These bastard molecules are something to think about in a preventative way, as well as a possible underlying cause of eczema or chronic cough or asthma issues. Seriously, I don't want you and your child wearing matching kerchiefs over your faces on play dates, just awareness (and relocation from your moldy home if you have one).

Mold is not just from old wet houses, but generally in the air. Think about how food left out, becomes moldy, in possibly, a couple of hours, to a couple of days. Babies can be allergic to, or have sensitivity to, breathing in this air-born fungi. More research is necessary to understand how babies are being affected by what they are breathing and absorbing through their skin. Remember the blood-brain barrier is open during the first six months and still developing and strengthening through early childhood. This means that mold can reach into places in the brain that are normally unreachable in adults.

SPECIAL NOTE: I work with a few clients who were exposed to toxic levels of mold. They developed anxiety and panic attacks post exposure, along with a host of other health problems with symptoms similar to autoimmune disorders. I theorize that if mold gets to the amygdala gland which is the emotional memory center and your fight or flight gland (please see coming sections on healing emotions for more information), there could be anxiety or heightened emotional states (thank you to a very special client for this information). More research needs to be conducted about how mold could be affecting behavioral, emotional and mental health problems. Please consult with a naturopath if you suspect this problem in your child.

NOTE: If you purchase non-organic produce, the mold in your refrigerator could contain pesticides and therefore all of your food will be exposed to a build-up of pesticides. You can give your fridge a cleaning with water mixed with vinegar and the essential oils, sage and lemon. Then, if you can, switch to organic produce only (while I do buy/pick mostly organic produce, to be completely honest, I don't clean my fridge like this … maybe I will now). I keep a clean house (or small apartment as is the case) sometimes the fridge, closet and my car (hybrid) aren't always as presentable. I am sure you are a great fridge cleaner!

Essential oils and mold: Essential oil use is one of the best ways I have come across to reduce mold toxicity. The highly anti-microbial, anti-bacterial, anti-fungal effects of certain oils provide a super clean for the inside of the body. Remember the story of the thieves who bathed themselves in oils and did not catch the plague.

Using oils that are safe for babies and toddlers are great, but children with higher sensitivities to mold may also require more thorough house cleaning. You can make your own cleaner using vinegar, clove, cinnamon, rosemary and clary sage. (**Unrelated tip:** cinnamon sprayed around the house, also keeps ants away, so does salt). Your homemade cleaner can be used to wash down walls, floors, toys and your babies' sleeping environments on a regular basis. Also, use a humidifier with five to ten drops of red thyme for a super anti-microbial cleaning at night (red thyme cannot be used on the skin, it's too strong). You can also make your own healing lotion, using an olive oil base or other oil base adding geranium, cinnamon, sage, lemon and eucalyptus. Then your baby can receive the benefits of stronger oils, through the breast milk. Please research what oils are safe for pregnant/nursing mothers, and what oils can be directly applied to babies and children, or consult with an aromatherapist.

We have so much power in maintaining the health of our children, and in creating an environment inside them, where healthy genes are chosen. Give it everything you've got, on every micro-level.

Search Item: Babies and mold inhalation. Essential oils to treat mold and air toxins. Effects of mold on the amygdala gland, the emotional memory center (as said above, highly emotional or out of control children could be dealing with mold in this center, of the brain).

Consult with a naturopath for mold allergy testing: If your child has eczema or a chronic cough, you may want to arrange an appointment with a naturopath for allergy testing.

21. LONG-TERM HEALTH and THE BLOOD-BRAIN BARRIER:

Blood-Brain Barrier Function: Just to help remind us (from section 2) … *The blood-brain barrier is the restraint mechanisms of cell junctions, between the blood and cerebrospinal fluid (CSF) (Sanders et al., 2012). Essentially, it is the wall that keeps unwanted molecules away, from the most important parts of the brain's functioning. In the article Barrier Mechanism in Developing Brains, it described the infant blood-brain barrier as "leaky" which "may render developing brains more vulnerable to drugs, toxins, and pathological conditions, contributing to cerebral damage, and later neurological disorders" (Sanders et. al, 2012).*

SPECIAL NOTE: As you know I am incredibly sensitive to chemicals, cell phones and so on. Now it could be as I previously said when I sounded like a total A-hole… "because I keep my system so pure, I can perceive toxins." Yes, I think this is true (and true of other pure system keepers) and … here's another theory. I have had a few things to deal with in the past seven or so years that could be labeled traumatic, leading to nightmares and anxiety not unlike symptoms of PTSD, which I managed with brain reprogramming (see final sections) and a little wine. High stress has a relationship with a weakened blood-brain barrier (please Google stress weakens blood-brain barrier). As said, in section 2, the central nervous system and blood-brain barrier are weakened when astrocytes become activated due to stress and toxins (Alvarez, J., Katayama, T. and Prat, A., 2013).

About three years ago, I began having some mild Lyme disease-like symptoms, such as sleep issues, joint pain, heart pain, brain fog and hypersensitivity even though I have never been bit by a tick (I find it very hard to believe that with my sensitivity that I would not have known it). I was also tested for Lyme disease which came back negative. In the past eight weeks, I have been treating myself with homeopathy (Celletech's Tick 1, Tick 2 and Ledum) and my symptoms have decreased. So I believe that I had a weakened blood-brain barrier (from stress and trauma) which may have allowed mycoplasmas (which can be co-infections of Lyme into important parts of my brain) thereby disrupting my nervous system. (Don't worry, the brain reprogramming has kept me functioning very well through the years, and now with a more peaceful life situation, a few nutritional and supplement additions, I am actually feeling very strong and well.) (Further, I believe I am led to certain experiences, paths and information by that very large personal team of Archangels, for the purpose of my role as a mother, writer and therapist. Thanks, Archangels!)

*****In a study that looked at persons with traumatic brain injury, a breakdown of the blood-brain barrier and oxidative stress is linked to neurological problems associated with TBI. Basically, it is not just the head injury but … what gets inside the head BECAUSE of the injury (Readnower, RD et al., 2010).

*****From Public Health Alert … Chronic Lyme patients and Gulf War Veterans have something in common … they have or can have a mycoplasma infection, the type … mycoplasma fermentans. Mycoplasma fermentans is also linked to Fibromyalgia, Multiple Sclerosis and Rheumatoid Arthritis and … biological warfare (www.publichealthalert.org/mycoplasma). So commonly known diseases have something to do with what is in the air and water! I wonder if all of these increasing problems with

autoimmune disorders are initiated by mycoplasmas. I also wonder if these persons with autoimmune disorders may have had a weakened blood-brain barrier to start with, making them more susceptible to the aforementioned infection? *****Disturbances of the blood-brain barrier are associated with autoimmune disorders (Alvarez, J., Katayama, T. and Prat, A., 2013).

*****Right now a blood-brain barrier has an extremely big job to do, and it likely the reason that everyone knows someone, who has an autoimmune disorder or cancer. How we care for our young, our water, our air, our forests and our bodies, is how we change that. Scientifically speaking, the functions of the earth are not separate from your physiological system. This is not a new age concept, like "we are all one" (I am not getting down on "we are all one" or anything). I'm just saying it is inarguable that our cells are molecularly a part of the ecosystem of the planet. Please teach your children to be grateful for the molecular environment of Mother Earth and that if we harm her, we harm ourselves.

Standard care procedures and trauma could cause a weakened blood-brain-barrier: I hypothesize that problems with an improperly developed blood-brain barrier can in part be sourced from early childhood standard care procedures such as ultrasounds, birthing procedures and vaccines, along with gross food, toxins or emotional trauma, resulting in possible health problems in childhood (or down the road), such as asthma, eczema, autoimmune disorders, cancer and allergies. If a child's blood-brain barrier does not fully develop or is weakened from a physical or emotional trauma, all kinds of particles as said above can pass through to parts of the brain, where you just don't want them to go. The difference between a healthy blood-brain barrier and non-healthy one is like sand being thrown at your eyes with sunglasses covering them or sand being thrown at your eyes taped open. Now imagine oxidants, radiation and mycoplasmas getting past the not-yet-developed or traumatized blood-brain barrier. The astrocytes are freaking out because there is almost always a toxic overload, immune system and stress cycle almost always turned on, then inflammation and an environment for unhealthy gene codes to be expressed and then, disease. So depressing, right? Maybe throw the book down here. No don't … let's vision something different.

Strong healthy blood-brain barrier: Now imagine a completely strong and healthy blood-brain barrier that came from healthy organic food/superfoods, love, a natural birth, a co-sleeping bond and from essential oil protection, herb strength and homeopathic immunization. Astrocytes are resting, calm and communicating production of everything in harmony and balance, like neurotransmitters and happy hormones. The pineal gland is practically star-shaped and sending sparkling life rhythms. Now, your child does not have to spend so much time fighting particles in their internal environment and can spend their energy on being happy, healthy and imaginative (then grow up and resolve the environment for the rest of us assholes!). Oh, I'm sorry was that offensive? Really, not you individually, it was meant in a collective we-really-need-to-care-sort-of-way. I know you do!

22. PLAY, TOYS, THE TOOTH FAIRY AND THE SENSES:

It is very, very important to keep sacred your child's space of play. If they are creatively engaged in something **please, please** don't interrupt them ... if at all possible. As parents, we have been taught to ask our children questions about what they're doing (thinking that we are connecting or giving attention) when they are in the middle of creating an entirely new society with a couple of sticks and a ribbon. It can actually be better (whenever possible) to let them be. What they are creating in their brains when they are in the midst of imagination, are the connections that they will build on for intelligence and the ability to focus. If they receive frequent interruptions, there are frequent interruptions in the way their brain makes connections. Uh, sometimes this cannot be helped, like the above-mentioned child hunkered down in a family of six ... uninterrupted play, not happening too much. Whatever you can do to allow your children to think on their own, for as long as possible, is really important and it also how they form their own self-concept. (This does not mean that you don't talk to your child, ask questions or give lots of loving attention, it just means when they are playing please recognize that it is like the Dalai Lama in the middle of prayer, it is not a good time to ask him if he would like some peaches.)

Even when you have a newborn, it's important to have a philosophy in mind about their future play, as well as, the kind of toys you want your infant, toddler and child to work with. It will take time to establish with family members and friends (who want to buy all kinds of gifts), what your position is on the subject. People are generous and have their own ideas about what it means to have toys as a child. So you will have to be clear and strong about what you think on this issue. There are lots of ways that family and friends can collaborate with you and have a very special relationship with your child. Again, setting the groundwork for what you believe is best in food, television exposure and toys will be necessary in order to get everyone in your child's life on the same page.

Simpler toys make more brain connections: Consider toys that really allow the imagination to fly, toys that are props for the drama that's unfolding in your child's mind. Avoid toys that do all the entertaining for your child in ten seconds so that they move onto the next entertaining thing. I am referring to all that bling, bling, beep, beep, battery operated stuff. That zero to seven brain development is critical, and play that is initiated through your child's imagination is what makes the connections for greater learning and intelligence. If they are spoon-fed imagination and entertainment, there are less brain connections of their own. The brain connections become media driven or driven by the thoughts of popular culture. Give them a chance to show you what they were born with, rather than what they become programmed with. Plus simpler toys in which the child is responsible for initiating the ideas, means it is more likely that they will play for longer and on their own. They won't be accustomed to standing down from their own ideas while something else is creating for them. They will be responsible at an early age to be their own creators. Give this to them, it is their right!

*****I really tried to go as natural as possible, with regards to toys, with not complete success, but mostly. When my daughter was a newborn, silk scarves were tied to a ceiling fan so that she could watch the colorful fabric spinning. Infant toys for my daughter included wooden rattles and drums. Bowls, spoons and water were especially fun for her. At age one she could spend an hour investigating the contents of the recyclables. Don't be afraid to let them play in the dirt!

Search Items: Montessori and Waldorf Philosophy (Gives great ideas for household set up and toys that provide optimal learning and development.)

No buying toys at the grocery store rule: Consider what happens when you buy a toddler an item at the grocery store on one trip and then say no on the following trip. It's like building a house next to a live volcano … it's just not a good idea. What I mean is … when you buy a two year-old a toy while you are at the grocery store, the next time you go the store, it is very hard for them to handle "not this time." I think they literally foam at the mouth when they expect something and then don't get it. I really tried hard to stick to this, "no buying toys at the grocery store rule" and it generally made shopping with my daughter much easier. If I wanted to get her something, I surprised her on a different occasion. Now it should be said, that none of these situations went perfectly for me. I just hoped to share something that might make it easier for you. I could tell you about the major all-out tantrum over a shiny pink balloon, but I won't. I didn't have the opportunity to shop without my child mostly, but if you do, it is best.

SPECIAL NOTE: People have used the term "spoiled" when referring to children who have been over-bought material items. Spoil means to ruin. They don't need tons of things and they don't need relationships based on being given everything they become groomed to be addicted to. Give them your time, your love, your creativity … this will never ruin them.

With all of this said, and my great efforts at avoiding over-materialization, it turns out we all like things. And well, it's fun to shop sometimes. I don't always want to sit in the woods. I want to buy a new sweater. One day, my daughter (age six at the time) and I were hitting the stores, getting new items for our apartment. Every store we went to, my daughter got a new item, craft, reading chair and so on. She still was not happy, launching into the child "I want more" scenario. It's really a sickness. Finally, I had had it! I began some ridiculous tirade about being grateful and probably brought up dying children in developing countries. Finally, I asked (I mean told) her to spend some time in her room to think about this, while I cooled down. After some time, she called me in, asked me to sit on her bed, told me to take a deep breath. She then asked me to imagine my favorite beautiful place. What immediately sprung inside my frustrated head was, "I am at a bar, I'm drinking, smoking (Natural American Spirit tobacco), laughing with friends" (which was me, fifteen years ago or maybe less). My daughter then said, "Do you feel better now." "I DO feel better," I replied. I then took myself out of the bar (of my mind) and into the present, where we agreed to list all the things we're grateful for. This problem (I want more and don't feel satisfied) never comes up in the woods.

Nature is the best play: Gardens and items in nature are the absolute best connectors of creativity, intelligence and soul. Give as much opportunity for that wisdom and flow of the natural world to enter their consciousness. Take them to as many places as you can where there are no toys, no other choice, but the ample props of story and creation placed in the woods, by rivers, ponds, lakes, by the ocean, at the base of a tree and inside a mud puddle. This is where the greats of the world are made! Think about how nature weaves a very intricate system of life with incredible details. Whatever you are close to, you absorb.

Say yes to play, as often as you can: When your child asks you to play, say "Yes" whenever you can. I attempt to follow this, but in full disclosure, I really don't always feel like getting down on the ground, pretending my tiny Lego person has a tray of pink sparkle cupcakes for the tiny Lego neighbor. I am as honest as possible, with my daughter. In the kindest of ways, I have asked her if she ever sees adults playing those sorts of games, to which, she replied no. I told her that when you get older, you like to play different sorts of things (like late night dancing with salt, lime and tequila drunk from the belly buttons of strangers … you can throw the book on the floor now!). Glad you decided to pick it back up! Anyway, since it's been just the two of us, I am, at times, my daughter's playmate. So, we have come to some great compromises. We often play a dramatic game called "coffee shop" and we both love it! I show up or she shows up at the coffee shop, and we are all, "Hey how are you?" and "What are you up to these days?" Sometimes, she's a scientist, in a ballet troupe, a college student or has just had a new baby. I can be in the kitchen for this game, doing dishes or actually drinking coffee. It's great! **In contradiction to what I just said:** I equally think that children sincerely benefit from playing on their own (as said in the beginning of this section). So, my saying, "say yes as often as possible" is not that often or in theory they are so creatively engaged, that they rarely ask you, so when they do, you say yes. Now, I have confused you. How about … everything in balance!

Play-based learning: I know that there is a ton of pressure to have your children learning sight words by age four or five (and in every possible extracurricular activity … different topic I know, but I think play trumps tennis lessons). Play-based learning creates the strongest brain connections. Then, when it's time for them to actually read or do more academic or other tasks (and they are ready), they will be doubly equipped. Please research.

Tooth Fairy: When my daughter began losing teeth (age six), one of her peers got an American Girl Doll for the first lost tooth. "What?!!!" I thought, "Now the rest of us parents are totally screwed." My daughter will find a dollar under her pillow and think, "Gosh, my tooth fairy is kind of stingy, little Betsy, gets an American Doll and I get a green piece of currency with an ugly, old president on it." We must develop some sort of parent tooth fairy code with a one to five dollar limit or something. If we don't, it will seem like Santa and the Tooth Fairy like rich kids better. Also on this topic, my daughter asked me directly, if I was the tooth fairy. I didn't want to lie, and so I told her. Then she wanted the truth about the Easter Bunny. Thank God, she stopped before we got to Santa. If there is someone I want to keep, it's him.

Senses: The senses mean so much to a child's state of well-being, especially since so much of childhood is not tangibly remembered. Smells, sounds and lights could illicit life-long feelings of happiness, like when I smell Rave Hairspray (please don't use Rave, please get a natural/organic hairspray), it reminds of the eighties, a pink mini skirt and a date with a sixteen year-old boy that I had been majorly crushing on. He was really cute … but OK, back to the present. You know what I mean when I talk about the senses taking you places, right?

Anyway, I have two salt lamps on constantly in the home and they are so peaceful in any room! I often light a candle at bedtime or we have occasional candlelight dinners. We have had sunrise mornings in our car at the beach with our poetry notebooks out, and recently attended a candlelit labyrinth walk in the woods. There have been many, many walks through flower gardens, smelling and absorbing color. We keep a singing bowl in the home, along with plenty of other instruments. Music of any kind (maybe not heavy metal until they're an angry teen), is a life raft! I don't think there is anyone who has been more impressed with my hip hop stylin' than my daughter. If all else if failing, a dance party in the kitchen, always wins!

Essential oils, boiling herbal teas, the making of raw chocolate (baby daddy – raw chocolatier), and of course, the general baking and cooking have been regular important smells that I dearly hope, will bring my daughter comfort through her life. Trees, water, rocks, shells, dirt and sand have also been a major part of experiencing the senses. Oh gosh, I almost forgot about painting! … but you already knew that one. We have frequented art shows, museums, drum circles and music venues together. Wow, I sound like a really great mom right?! (Please read later sections on emotions and brain reprogramming to get a more balanced perspective of me and I sometimes yell and do bad parenting things that I feel guilty about.) **Note:** Having fun and appealing to the senses is a way to override the unavoidable challenges of being a growing human and having total responsibility for a growing human.

23. STRUCTURE:

Order and structure are essential in the early years of your child's life. For myself, I had to learn this lesson the hard way. As a self-professed, free spirit, moving about from place to place, experiencing new people, jobs and creative expressions, structure was not exactly in my signature. With a newborn and infant, this fly by the seat of your pants mentality can actually work in your favor because you are at the mercy of your baby's biological flow. Any structure you create may be replaced in a week, day or minute. Your structure might be something like, "I make decaf coffee at some point in the morning, breastfeed, I take the dog outside (if you have one), then breastfeed again, and then, while breastfeeding, ponder for a bit about staying in pajamas, or actually getting dressed."

Somewhere around a baby's six month mark, you can find a regular way of being, which psychologically makes a difference (mostly for you). After having to wing our own very basic biological needs in the newborn stages, we cling to this Mr. Roger's, change your shoes every time you come in the door routine. Children thrive on the comfort of regularity, knowing what comes next, means they feel secure. When they feel secure, they internalize the confidence that security brings. You are their navigator, their legs, their communicator and their director. When you feel strong and comfortable, they feel strong and comfortable. Giving yourself a daily path to follow, with room for flexibility, helps you to be this for them.

As infants grow into toddlers, everything changes. You move from nurturer to dictator (hopefully a kind and loving one), and if you don't make the shift, you will get toppled like I did. At this stage, they need you to pull out your big alpha guns, set up some hard and fast rules that rarely get broken, and say "no" and mean it. With that set-up, you can then honor the spirit of your child, inside the safe container that allows one to grow, with total trust. It is the cross between old school parenting (without physical discipline) and the newer models of respecting the child as a unique person, with a very real purpose.

When my daughter was very young, I was really too flexible, saying, "oh what's the big deal, she wants to play with that frying pan hanging on the wall" and so on. While I was, in actuality, setting boundaries (mostly), I was not always stating the boundaries as simply and as consistently, as children really need it to be. I thought I was respecting my daughter, by explaining things in lots of detail, when clear and direct, is what she needed. I thought this type of parenting could create a person who was so honoring of their own being because I was so honoring her with explanation of why she couldn't touch the light socket. What I had to learn was that she required the structure of "clear and simple" to be solid in herself. The truth is I lacked authority in myself and self-authority in a parent, is how a child imprints self-authority into their life. For lack of a better term, I was getting "forced" to evolve into my own strength by my screaming toddler.

And so, as my daughter grew into toddlerhood, my flexible rules were too ambiguous. She would tantrum at any limits being set, and I, this seemingly calm, flowing, attempting to negotiate individual, was getting her ass kicked. Finally, I was educated by my daughter's principal at her Montessori school, who said to me, in the loveliest of Irish accents "If you've said no, Kate, stick to your no. Even if you think you should have said yes, stick to what you've said." This changed everything about the authority and strength in me, and therefore, in my daughter.

SPECIAL SIDE NOTE: I don't agree with spanking children because I don't agree with physical discipline. Mostly my beef with this ... if a circumstance has gotten to the point of spanking, the parent is probably so pissed off that spanking is not a conscious form of behavior correction, it's chosen because things feel out of control. Don't get me wrong, I have felt out of control as a parent and behaved badly. I get it. However, I think if spanking is not in the mix of parent OK things to do, we are not likely to go for it when we are in the middle of a family shit show. We might just swear, rant, walk away and then apply some reasonable consequences ... now you all know what I do (sometimes). My daughter generally thinks at this point that swearing is funny, but if I spanked her she would be traumatized. So yeah, just don't spank.

Authority in balance/parent tool box: Please take the following authority segment in balance. Ignoring negative behaviors and applying positive praise of good behaviors are still super, super important tactics. Distraction is another key; i.e. toddler is throwing food at your dog and you begin dancing, waving your arms and singing so that they shift their focus. Try not to say "stop that" all day. I think the authority is a presence you carry as firm around you both, and applies itself mainly when things have to get done, like getting shoes on because you have to leave. Creating games and making things exciting can be incorporated in this as well; i.e. "Quick, quick get your shoes, there is a helicopter outside and we must evacuate due to a category five hurricane" ... well maybe not this dramatization for a two year old, maybe eight year old. Create a parent tool box and know when to apply, which is frankly accomplished by trial and error.

Authority choice and internalized order: Basically, you are making the decisions, and giving some choice inside it, for example, "It's time to get dressed," there is no choice in that, but, "Which of these three shirts, would you like to wear?"... the child's choice inside your decision. If your child convinces you that it is not time to get dressed, then you lose the authority. If you have said so, stick to it. If they convince you to go apple picking instead of blueberry picking, that's different and an area when a child could choose. In listening to others share their knowledge and experiences, I have learned that if you don't provide the limits during these early years, children will lack internalized order for themselves (meaning your structure and self-authority are how children cellular imprint self-authority, order and boundary for themselves). Then at the next stage of development (if parent self-authority has been lax ... please don't be hard on yourself, if this is so) between the ages of seven to twelve, you will be attempting a more difficult task of employing structure. And if you skip this next phase, by the teenage years, it's pretty much, too late. **Note:** I spent some time working with teenagers at a special education school. I actually love teenagers and do not think it is ever too late. It is just that things could go easier, if you get the structure in the beginning. Most of the teenagers that I worked with had a history of chaotic and/or abusive home lives related to their emotional and learning problems, so no structure definitely equaled problems.

Choose clear related consequences: I have learned that it's important to be clear about consequences, and make them as logical as possible. If your child throws a ball across the room, you will not want to repeat, "Don't do that" five times. Then you feel pushed to the point of yelling and possibly employing an obscure, unrelated consequence because you're upset (I have done this). Simply take the ball away and tell them that the ball is only used outside. Then stick to it. When there is a behavior, connect the consequence to it, so it has meaning to the child, and relates to a possible "next circumstance." For example, if your child is refusing to leave the library and you've tried all of your tactics, like "Let's go take out the books" or "Come on, we are going home for a yummy lunch," then go strong and clear and mean it. "I am counting to three, and if you don't leave then, we will not take out these books." Choose clear, related consequences, and always follow through. This changed who I was as a parent and then, my daughter settled. Once you have set up some laws that your household can live by, you can then provide freedom, creativity and that honoring of soul.

Create a rule or structure: If something is driving you nuts, like some sort of repetitive behavior, it is usually an indication that a rule or structure needs to be created. For example, my daughter required repeated reminders to do basic things before school, getting dressed, hair brushing and so on. Me, overwhelmed and insane about asking again and again. Then, me making a list of morning responsibilities, giving it to her, with a clear natural consequence (no playtime because list is not finished) and reward (more play-time because list is finished): problem solved. Say to yourself, "OK, this is making me crazy, I need a law, a structure or a rule." Keep in your mind, "There is always a solution." **Note:** Parents have told me that shifting the responsibility to their child, as in giving them a list of their a.m. and p.m. tasks that they accomplish, has really helped improve household peace and increase child responsibility. I hope it can work for you as well.

System can make things feel less personally upsetting: If you create a system that the family relies on, age appropriate expectations, chores/tasks, natural consequences and rewards as part of the system, the whole parent/child relationship becomes so much less personal. Meaning, if you are asking your child one hundred times to do something, you are just building bitterness. How could you not? If children are responsible to the system of lists, natural consequences and natural rewards, that you both can lean on it, rather than the intense emotion of this parent/child epidemic of "parent repeating request, child not doing" then the relationship is theoretically better.

Make a specific request for the positive behavior you want: Along with your system and authority, try to ignore what you can in negative behavior (in balance), and praise the heck out of the good stuff, as said above. Please look into The Kazdin Method of Parenting, for more information on this. This method really supports clear directions about the behavior you want: i.e. "Please put your feet flat on the floor" vs. "Stop putting your feet on the table" or "Please speak kindly" vs. "Stop being so rude." (I am working on this myself ... it definitely runs counter to impulse.) This method also suggests that praise should not be arbitrary, but very specific to the behavior: i.e. "You did such a great job folding your clothes and putting them away" vs. "You're so totally awesome," though I think you might randomly tell your kid they're totally awesome on occasion. But, as far as reinforcing goes, specific praise is where it is at!

24. BODY BOUNDARIES:

Please teach your child self-love and respect for their body at an early age. Certainly all the safety talk about how and who can touch your child's body is very important. In addition, be aware of how adults interact with your child. I have witnessed good people unconsciously exhibit poor boundaries with children, which is confusing and potentially damaging to a child's psychological understanding of what it means to have personal authority. For example, I have seen adults wrestle or tickle a child without respecting a child's discomfort or, not stop when the child says so. The child learns that they are powerless to create a limit for their personal space, possibly growing into an adult who gives themselves away or crosses the boundaries of others. I have witnessed adults take tickling liberties with children they don't know very well, again a real violation of a child's boundary, which sends a message that a child should allow any adult to touch their body. If you wouldn't go up to an adult that you are just meeting at a party and begin touching or tickling, then it is not OK to do to a child.

I have also seen poor boundary issues translate in child to child situations. While children have natural sexual feelings as young as toddlerhood, children are not equip to handle any touching between their peers, in my opinion. There are accepted concepts like "exploration" and so on, but I feel that you cannot know where the motivation to explore is coming from or, where it will go or what is going on in the other child's family. Sexual trauma can probably be found in anyone's family history and even if there is not current abuse, genetics are running to be chosen. If exploration or otherwise occurs in a frequent way, then a child could become sexualized at an early age or may tap into that old sexual abuse family history floating around in almost everyone's human body (possibly in the form of junk DNA) which could distort, who the child could be.

In addition, men addicted to pornography has become so problematic on so many levels (please read the Time Magazine March 2016 issue on this), but in the case of your energy absorbing child, it could be detrimental. Remember, the glial cells and the parent/child glial cell connection and anything in proximity to your child's glial cells. Deeply connected love-making is a wonderful vibration (privately in your bedroom or in your living room because you have a co-sleeper in your bed), and sexual addiction is well, not that. I have seen children act out gross sexual energy, when there is no sexual abuse occurring. Unfortunately, even in the best of families, addiction to pornography is accepted, almost like a cultural high five. Because of parent/child energy exchanging and parent/child imprinting, a child "exploring" with another child may be bringing this family problem into the situation. **Note:** I am not against porn or other ways in which people explore their sexuality or enjoy their sexuality, but there is loving adult exploration, liberation and pleasure and then there is gross addiction which is not sexuality, it is sickness.

Some of the motivation for child exploration may not be sexual at all, but may be intertwined within other sorts of issues. For example, my daughter and two other female peers, agreed to show each other their underwear. Pretty harmless right? The same female peer then "told" them to show their "privates." Both my daughter and the other female peer said no. Could be just curiosity, but the commanding six year old female peer is in fact, a bit bossy and insists on her way, in a lot of other situations. This peer is also highly interested in how she looks and has said that she wants to impress boys with her outfits (maybe media driven acculturation). Anyway, it's possible that the female peer's motivation was about control or otherwise, hard to say, right? But, if my daughter had given into that command because she felt she had to, there is potentially a loss of personal authority. My daughter said no, because I have been clear with her that she should say no in these situations. This is not an area for ambiguity because it's hard enough, for adults to decipher people, please don't place the burden on your child.

As said above and one more time for good measure, it is hard to determine between genuinely being curious and all of the other emotional connecting points to boundaries, control and sexuality in families. It is not to say that your child won't change in front of another child or should hide or should feel any shame about the body, but there is a distinction to make. Speak frankly, about the distinction. It is ok say to say vagina and penis. It is Ok to speak frankly about being naked, honoring the body and as well as creating a boundary for self. This is not about body guilt and shaming, it is about having self-authority and liberation. However, if the authority is taken, there is guilt and depending to what degree the authority is taken, possibly other issues as well.

SPECIAL NOTE: If your child tells you something is going on, please, please respond to what they are saying immediately. Protect your child's body boundary. I believe loss of it, is responsible for generations of people who cannot actualize their self-value in the world. If you have a gut feeling about something, don't worry about offending someone, follow it.

Tell your child that their body is theirs and it is beautiful: While children have natural sexual feelings, they cannot be put in situations that their age cannot handle. I tell my daughter that her body is beautiful and sacred and no one else can touch her body. I tell her that she can touch her own body and that it is her right, and no one else's right. I have explained that when people are older and (possibly) in a relationship, people like to touch each other's body and it is beautiful and OK … but like wine, which is really wonderful, it is not for children.

Support body connection: Once you have set a firm boundary inside and around your child, please find ways that they can honor and connect to their awesome non-puritanical body. Things like dance, belly dancing, yoga, maybe swimming in the nude, martial arts and healthy wrestling with your child (where they set the limit and you listen) are important. To allow healthy curiosity, you might let them look at 14th and 15th century art, where the naked body is depicted with beauty; i.e. Michelangelo's *The David* (between you and me, and NOT in conversation with your curious child, David is a biblical hottie!) Anyway, one last thing … check out Amy Cuddy on YouTube, she teaches power poses (like the hand on hips "Wonder Woman" pose) that lowers stress chemicals and increases positive hormone release. You can try these on for yourself and with your children, especially your girls. When I first taught my daughter the power pose she said, "Mom, I am already so powerful, if I do this I might rip out a tree!" OK then, lesson over.

25. CHILD FEELINGS:

So my daughter is about two years old, all of the leggings, those soft lovely pants are dirty. It is 7:25 a.m., I need to leave in five minutes. My daughter will not put anything else on, and is screaming and yelling, crying and upset. Jeans just won't cut it. I am kind of freaking out myself, because if I don't leave in those five minutes, she will be late for school and I, for work. This is the moment when your yoga friend wants to tell you to take a deep breath, and you want to tell her to take her downward dog and, well, shove it up her very firm .... OK, we'll stop there (downward dog is actually one of my favorite poses). Anyway, with that said, I know that my agenda does not mean that my daughter's feelings aren't real or justified to her ... and I still need to leave in five minutes. To avoid disasters such as this, structure, as said above, is really your best bet ... like an outfit, which includes leggings, laid out the night before.

Well ... things weren't perfect (at the time, I lived in a tiny apartment with a broken washing machine) even though perfect is what I really wanted. And ... these are opportunities to teach children about feelings. Not only teach, but recognize children as people who are really legitimately upset sometimes. When my daughter was calm (and me too), I went back to her (and still do), to talk about, or at age two, draw about, or role play about, the feelings that she went through in the intense "I want leggings!" moment or the many others that followed. Sometimes we would come up with structural solutions together or a different way to think about it, or just a mutual set of apologies for our collective freak out. Children have intense feelings and then come to conclusions on their own, like "Mommy is just mean," and is not letting me wear leggings or otherwise. It's important to hear their feelings (when the situation is over and calm) and also help them to see the perspective of what occurred, more widely, so they are not left secretly hating you. If you leave them alone with their perceptions, then it is possible that when they're a teenager, and all those glial cells are turning over resurfacing early childhood emotions, you might get a whole lot of slamming doors and "you are the worst parent in the world" sort of madness. (I'm a little nervous that I have that coming. Maybe my daughter will read the book just before puberty hits, taking pity on my fumbling as a parent.)

Feeling books and scales: Child feeling picture books can be introduced as early as nine months old, and can be referred to throughout the day. Children as young as three, four and five, can use feeling scales. You draw a picture of a face demonstrating a feeling, such as shy, mad, sad, embarrassed, guilty, excited and so on, then make a scale of one to ten beneath it. You can ask about a multitude of situations, finding out how high or intense the feeling was for them in any given situation, then discuss ideas to make things easier or tools to handle emotions. If, for example, you are addressing your child's anger, you can say, "How high up the scale did your anger go?" (about not being able to play outside or whatever the situation). You can say, "What did you do when you were mad? Then what happened? Next time please tell me that you're mad, and we can think of a solution" instead of throwing my most precious vase against the wall. I am using sarcasm because I'm of Irish descent, from the Northeast and hoping to make you laugh, but I am not recommending that you really use sarcasm with your young child. It can be confusing and hurtful. Humor yes!, anywhere you can.

Be as gentle as you can when children are having feelings: Some feelings are simply given the space to be felt. Some feelings may feel out of control to you and your child. Sometimes structure and direction help give a child a reason to switch from the fight or flight response, and strengthen the override developing in their frontal lobe (see more in later sections on emotions and the amygdala gland). For example, if you say, "If you don't calm down, we will not be able to join our friends playing in the park, we will have to go home." you will help them to think as opposed to being swamped with emotion. Sometimes providing authority and a specific limit helps a child to learn the skill of overriding negative or flooding emotion. You may add (to show honor for the feeling), "I hear that you felt angry about having to wear boots when you wanted to wear sandals" (on a snowy freezing cold day). Having tools to deal with emotions is another key, kind of like distraction. In the case of this situation you can say "Let's take a deep breath, jump up and down ten times, get a hug, throw those boots on and join those other two-year old turkeys."

There will be other circumstances, when you'll just need to hold and hug them through the emotion, particularly during the ages of two and three. I was honestly not always great at this, sometimes, but mostly I wanted the screaming, yelling and whining to stop, because it was triggering the heck out of me (please see later sections on healing emotions). If you can gently hold them through until they can talk, draw, role play or puppet out what happened, I believe your child will grow more confidently and peacefully without issues of appeasing your inability to take it. Sincere good luck with this, and please create a blog and do a series of youtube specials, if you master this. Uh, if you Google my name, you will not find such a blog or youtube special.

Day-to-day can build a pattern of anger between child and parent(s): This year at Montessori School, a peer taught my daughter how to use the middle finger. I am pretty sure I have been flipped off for all the asking you have to do as a parent (in repetition) to get the basic stuff done, "brush your teeth," "please clean up," "time to go," "time for bed," "no you can't do that," "please get dressed," "please put your feet down," "please quiet down," etc. Frankly, I don't blame my daughter for being upset and I don't blame me either ... we've got to get this stuff done, right? It is frustrating on both ends and as they grow, they want to be independent and they STILL, want you to clean up after them. Other than some lists and structure, laughing and creativity, I have not found a way to completely avoid this "child annoyed with parent, parent annoyed with child" in the day-to-day responsibilities. I am working on it!

So sometimes, you have to get down on the floor and get at these built-up feelings. Recently, after a day of frustrating comments exchanging between myself and my daughter, we got down on the floor. We did some growling and repeating of "I'm mad at you" back and forth. After about the fourth go of it, my daughter crawled over on my lap and said, "Mommy." We then just hugged each other for a while. Independence, nurturance, duty and love, it is quite a balancing act. Coming back to gratitude really helps.

Yelling is OK?: Believe it or not, sometimes you raising your voice, with a very firm and stern directive, is what is needed to stop a child from becoming out of control, inside an emotion (which strengthens their override abilities in the frontal lobe). As a parent, you are up against genetic history and current culture, and you must be the stronger element to these forces so that your child can be the highest and best expression of themselves. Simply said (with care and a bit of caution), sometimes (when not out of control), yelling is helpful!

Be strait with your kids: As your children develop more and more reason, tell them the truth about behaviors and feelings whenever you can. Talk to them like a person who you expect to be full of kindness, creativity and responsibility. When they don't do the right thing, tell them clearly, and then let them know that they are full of strength and good things, and that doing the wrong thing doesn't match who they are. Let them know that you see always, their best self and firmly (and sometimes passionately) tell them that the negative behavior is not of them. For example, "You are a person who is strong and kind. You are not someone who does not care for others. Let's help you find your way back to that person who is kind." When things are not addressed or a parent is overly critical, I believe we make narcissists. Love and truth is the way to a centered, balanced individual. **Note:** It's really hard not to talk to children with a change in tone and perspective (different from how you talk to other adults). However, I believe that if we shift (to a degree) our way of speaking to children, into speaking with them as fellow humans who we honor for their unique intelligence, children will grow with the idea of themselves as more capable.

26. INDEPENDENCE:

At age each age and stage, children are expanding emotionally, mentally and physically and well, spiritually too! If you are exceptionally agitated or gasping from whatever your once loving child just said to you, it could be a signal to birth a law and structure as said in previous sections. It can also be signaling an individuation between you and your child, from the previous stage of development in which they agitate to receive more independence. Montessori has got it right when they promote the notion that whatever your child is capable of doing, let them do it. A two year old, can bring their plate to the sink, choose their own outfit, prepare food, help put their clothes away and clean up after themselves. So imagine what a five year old can do. At age 7 and since age 5, my daughter has been responsible for doing her own laundry start to finish, including folding and putting away (with less support as she grows). She sweeps after dinner, helps load the dishwasher and is allowed to cross the street to a friend's house (which she feels so proud of).

Independence and self-responsibility are critical in the development of children, so they can differentiate between your thinking and theirs. Don't get me wrong, you are still the loving alpha captain that demonstrates authority, so that your child knows how to hold authority within. You can support that they have an opinion that you honor, even though you are in most situations the final decision-maker. They will likely get mad at you sometimes, which at first might feel bad but, it can be how they differentiate into who they are. For example, your child may want to go swimming at the lake, and you say no because its dinner time or you have a pile of laundry to do. If they are under the age of five, this could result in parent bashing or a tantrum. And while this is challenging, children learn that they have a different agenda, which means that they are now different from you. This is critical in the strengthening of a child's personal authority. As infants and even very young children, the connection to their parents (especially the mother) feels indistinguishable. The agitation is sometimes how they accomplish distinction.

You can be proactive about these developmental shifts, by lending support to their practice of differentiation. My daughter (for at least the past three years) sometimes asks me my opinion about what to wear. I support that it is her choice and typically when I do give my opinion about an outfit, she will almost always choose something different. Admittedly this has frustrated me (in the "why do you ask me?" sort of way), but I realized that she wants the opportunity to choose different from me (which is totally squashed and never allowed … I'm kidding). Again inside your structure and authority, recognizing and honoring their opinions or ideas as important and different from yours, will hopefully decrease their need to act out individuation negatively. Another important part of this process, is adding age appropriate responsibility as said above.

Keep the bond, and let them individuate: I think many a loving bond has been disrupted because the child can become so aggravating in their effort to separate (to expand into themselves) that you literally want to give them to a neighbor to finish the child-raising. The child says the most personal or hurtful things not necessarily consciously, but in a direct flow of evolution. The parent responds to these repeated insults by being pushed away and hurt. Success and individuation for the child! If we are more conscious of this, we can make planned rituals or, at the very least, feel less personally attacked by the little being we just poured our very blood, sweat and tears into … for months and years! Teenagers do this in big dramatic ways, but our little ones do this too. Let them go into the next phase, they can do it, they had You! to prepare them. **Note:** I have responded at times, in pretty ridiculous ways to these child-expansion insults like, "I do everything for you, I cook, I clean, I take you to your friend's house, I buy you …" this, that and so on. I hope you will learn from me and not do that (though teaching gratitude and showing real feelings when you are hurt are important). You are not meant to be your child's slave, but you have signed up for Sherpa duty. They want to take the next slope alone without us reminding them of how often we carried their bag. The bag carrying is tough sometimes.

27. COMMUNITY:

Being a stay-at-home mother or stay-at-home father, can be lonely at times. Everyone is so busy and fast, and you are running at a short-legged dog pace, compared to the Arabian horse race of society. Children do not move fast, nor do babies, for that matter. Getting out of the house with young children is like trying to get your eighty-year old Republican grandfather to admit that global warming is an actual scientific reality. You must be incredibly skillful or, just don't bother. With that said, connecting with others out of the house or inside your house is critically important to mental and emotional parent well-being. I found that having a connected group of mothers that I spent time with regularly, really made a difference in my experience. They were moving as loosely and sometimes as slowly as I was. They would agree to ball park appointment times at later hours, something like "I will meet you at the playground somewhere between 10 am and 11 am." When my daughter was an infant, I gathered with other mothers and we talked and nursed our babies. When my daughter was a toddler, we went to potlucks where she played with other children and I had interesting conversations with a variety of people. Now that my daughter is seven, we are a part of similar sorts of gatherings that keep us feeling like we're part of something.

I didn't always stay at home with my daughter and began working full-time when she was about two. No matter what your situation, working or not, gathering with others gives you an important connection, that builds comfort in you, through the sharing of experiences. If you don't have a group of friends readily available to you, there are all kinds of meet-up-groups for parents, or, you can visit the library. Other parents tend to be at the library with their kids, ready to meet people, too. Also, attending regular kid programs means that you can see the same faces and build from there. Having a child makes it easy to meet and talk with people ... it's like the single guy with a cute puppy. Suddenly there is a reason to say, "How old is he?" and "What's his poop schedule?" There are a lot of easy pick-up lines to choose from when approaching your potential new friend/parent. Don't be afraid to use them. Topics to approach include food, sleep, the ability to get a hairbrush through your child's hair, education, child's temperament and so on.

28. EDUCATION:

Making a decision about your child's education actually comes early on. You may get inklings about your child's style of being and learning within the first couple of years of their life. There are many options for matching who your child is, with a program that honors who they are.

There are Waldorf Schools, Montessori, Charter Schools, Wilderness Schools, Homeschooling and lots more. You are likely thinking that it's very costly to send a child to a private school, and you know what, it is! I live in a tiny apartment in part, so that I could afford to put my daughter in a Montessori School. I also received a fifty percent tuition scholarship. Maybe if you tell all of your friends about my book, I could buy a house, have the ability to pay full tuition and start on a college fund ... thanks so much, you rock! If you think public school is not the way to go for your child, please don't give up on an alternative way to give them what they best need. If you are OK with public school, but you're located in a public school district that you're not pleased with, don't be afraid to move. What happens in early education means that much! Please research. **Note:** The book has taken longer than I thought to write and life is changing with it ... so while I have been all about Montessori and certainly still sing its praises, I am going to be sending my daughter to public school next year. (Please <u>still</u> tell your friends about the book, I have college to pay for! and more importantly, we have the next generations to change!) I live in a great town, with a great public school and actually, it turns out my daughter does better with group learning (everyone working on the same thing), as opposed to the independent learning in Montessori. Go figure! Plus my daughter and her Montessori teacher were not exactly a match, it was kind of like Jane Goodall and Reese Witherspoon, hard to see them together for four years, if you know what I mean ... "Let's be quiet and study these majestic creatures" verses "I just want to talk to whomever is available about exuberant and vibrant things." (My daughter was compliant about her work, finishing it super fast, so that she could go off and be social ... not exactly Montessori style, but I gotta tell you, I love who she is!)

Montessori Education: My daughter has been to three Montessori schools ... uh, well, I moved around a lot (could be that free spirit/fear of commitment thing or following my right path), but that's a whole different topic, for a whole different book. Montessori has been a true gift, teaching us advanced potty training, order, responsibility, care for others, freedom of choice in learning materials, reading and so on. Maria Montessori is worth researching. She was brilliant, creating materials that advance five centers of the brain. Montessori is also worth reading about in designing your child's home life, even if they go on to a different type of education.
The following was pulled from www.womenofgrace.com/blog/?p=16584

"Followers of the Montessori method believe that a child will learn naturally if put in an environment containing the proper materials. These materials, consisting of 'learning games' suited to a child's abilities and interests, are set up by a teacher-observer who intervenes only when individual help is needed. In this way, Montessori educators try to reverse the traditional system of an active teacher instructing a passive class. The typical classroom in a Montessori school consists of readily available games and toys, household utensils, plants and animals that are cared for by the children, and child-sized furniture-the invention of which is generally attributed to Dr. Montessori. Montessori educators also stress physical exercise, in accordance with their belief that motor abilities should be developed along with sensory and intellectual capacities."

Again, Maria Montessori is so worth looking into, a super forerunner, with lots of guts. We are still benefiting!!!! Thank you. Thank you. Thank you.

Homeschooling: Homeschooling is not about toothless people who keep their kids home to muck up cow poop. Homeschooling has become a way that very progressive families foster, highly enriched development in their children. I recently learned of parents who quit their day jobs and built their work out of their home, so they could home school their very inventive and creative children. Sometimes, invention and creation get lost in public school standards. I always keep home schooling as an ace up my sleeve should I want, need or feel that it is best for my daughter.

My sister home schools her three lovely children and many friends in my community, do the same. They participate in super cool programming ... wilderness, circus, theater, dance, horseback riding, art, music and so much more. What I've noticed about children who have not been in an educational system, is their unmatched kindness and innocence, and the type of self-presence, we never want our children to lose. Don't get me wrong, I know amazing children educated in public school systems, and home school children with issues. It's just important to be open to the type of child you have, and the type of education they can handle, based on your gut feeling and life situation. If they're going to be labeled because they're the type of kid who cannot stay at a desk for a good portion of the day, please consider another way. I believe that flat, desk education will eventually be completely exchanged for movement, color, visual, and tactile learning that is natural to children. Many, many public schools are already taking great leaps. Yay, keep going!

Note: Please use **Gut + Research = Highest and Best Decision**, in choosing your child's education and don't be afraid to allow solutions and possibilities to emerge. You are not locked into anything!

SPECIAL NOTE: If your child is getting bullied at school or anywhere, you must stop it! Pull them out of wherever it's happening, or get in there and don't allow it. I have met with many in therapy on the other end of this. It really takes a toll on how a person develops and how their life turns out.

Apprenticeship/Purpose: Imagine what kind of people would inhabit the world, if at the very beginning of life, one's unique purpose was honored and lived. Finding my own value, mission and contribution has been such an ache in my heart. Even as a child, I was longing to grow up, so that I could do what I came to do. (If you read my book and possibly make a change in the life of your child, I will finally feel better, so thank you.) I think children should be invited on as board members for important organizations such as Green Peace or Save the Children. It would be great if they could have apprenticeships with doctors, herbalists, carpenters, firemen or veterinarians, depending upon their interest. When I pitched this to my daughter, she said she'd like to volunteer at a local music and art store (I'm working on it). My daughter also said that she would like to be an herbalist, and so we are planning time for a serious education with our local magic plant woman.

A conversation that you might have with your child in this regard … "(Insert Child Name), each of us comes to the planet earth for a very special reason, and we each have a very special purpose. I hope to help you honor yours and support it, even now. What do you think your special purpose is?" Most kids will have an answer and if they don't, say "no worries, we will find it together." **Brag Note:** My daughter recently said, "If I am going to be a nurse, I'll be Clara Barton, if I am going to be a writer, I'll be Rachel Carlson, if I am going to be an artist, I will be Van Gogh." "Just don't cut your ear off sweetie" I replied (I'm kidding). She then took a God pause (talking to God to find out who she will be) and said, "God says I will be a musician." She has read the young reader biographies of Clara Barton and Rachel Carlson, we have a slew of artist books in our home and my daughter takes guitar/keyboard lessons, but still pretty cool that she put it all together (little bit of mama bragging here, which we are entitled to, on occasion).

*****Deepak Chopra told his young children beginning at age four that they have a very special talent that no one else has and that this talent will serve humanity. He told them that they don't need to worry about grades in school or money or anything, only focus on their unique purpose in the world. His children ended up in the best schools, received top grades and have done financially well (Chopra, D., 1994).

29. THE SPIRITUAL SELF OF THE CHILD:

I'm just about ready to publish the book. The editing by my mother and my aunt finished weeks ago and I cannot seem to stop adding. I am worried that I won't tell you something important and you won't have what you need. Could you imagine if I didn't add this category? Anyway, I will stop the worry now and replace it with, "You are an amazing person, with strong instincts, a will to connect to the soul of your child and the impulse for their most beautiful life. You have everything you need and then some, in great and secure, loving abundance."

I won't talk long on this, because I HAVE to get the book to you. The spiritual self is the aspect of a person that is much larger than the day to day. It is the part of self that might stare at a jade plant for an hour and get a message to move to Vermont (that's me 2006). This part of the self could nurture itself as a Hindu, Christian, Muslim, Buddhist, Pagan or staring out at the vast ocean with a glass of wine (that might be my religion currently) (skip the wine with regards to your child). Though, I want to say, any aspects of religion that suppress women or tell them that they can't be leaders within that religion, should be aspects of that religion … not followed, in my opinion.

*****Rituals for blessing a new life are so beautiful, some sort of baptism. My daughter and I attended a deeply important baby blessing ceremony (when my daughter was two) which honored and cleared her spirit for an abundant life.

*****If you believe in past life and karma, please use an Emotion Code Therapist mentioned in section 3, to clear the miasmas (karmic patterns) for your child so they won't play out old difficult life schemes. Soooo much easier when you clear it all out!

Einstein and your child's energy field: Every person has a field of energy that they stand in and like love, you can't really see it, you feel it. You want your child to know their energetic field as part of their self-authority but also as a connection to the divine force of all things. You could break out a child's book on Einstein, showing them that everything is made of energy, including them. You could tell them that when they swim, they are part of the vast water and when they play in the mud, they are part of the deep richness of the earth. Tell them this extraordinary energy field is theirs and can be boundless, but can also have a boundary when it needs to. You can teach them to imagine/create a strong bubble around their field, made of steal and violet fire (or whatever you like), that only allows love to enter or be exchanged. **Note:** Children easily feel the feelings of others or energy field of others and sometimes are unable to differentiate between how they feel and how someone else feels … I have seen young children, including my own, act out someone else's dissonant energy/feelings/thoughts. Say to your child "You have your own sacred energy field and your job is to keep clear, light and loving and I will help you." Sometimes my daughter and I will say to each other, "You have funk on you" … which basically translates as "you are acting out energy or emotion that is not yours."

You can also teach them to ground their energy field:

1.) Have your child put their hand on top their head.

2.) Have them state their name, like "I am Kate."

3.) Say we are rooted like trees and have them repeat, "I am North, South, East, West aligned with the magnetic energy of the earth."

(This can work to chill out a wiry, out of sorts, or hyperactive child and can <u>keep</u> kids a little more chill, when done regularly.)

Energy, nature and grounding are *very* important topics of conversation with your child and hopefully interwoven in daily life (as in the exercises above). The spiritual self is something to listen to, honor and keep alive, amidst that competing energy of cultural pressure (which sometimes topples the true self). The earth is contained in a galaxy, in a Universe and there are countless Universes. It is all so, so vast and we have the availability to touch all of it, inside our cells (scientifically! and spiritually speaking). Don't let them forget!

*****Children will create endlessly … it is their piece of the Creator.

Take them to places that give them information, connection and ideas about how people honor the spiritual self: As I have said in previous sections and again in this one, probably to the point of annoyance, nature is the best connector of self. And, there are other supports that you may explore for the spiritual self of your child. When my daughter was an infant, we lived in "community" in Sedona, Arizona. Sedona is kind of a spiritual Mecca in the United States and millions travel there each year for this reason. Anyway, we lived in a mansion-type house shared with three other people as well as ourselves (me, baby daddy and daughter), overlooking a red rock canyon. The great room of our mansion-type house was used for tea ceremonies, healing workshops, poetry/singing event practice, drum circles/dancing and a dancing freedom workshop. Needless to say, my daughter was crawling through all of it, imprinting and absorbing the people, the joy, the spirit and the intelligence of these moments. **Side note:** About "living in community" … I have been accused of being a hippie, which is a real honor. But, I think because of how I dress and a few other lifestyle differences, I may be better categorized as a classic tree-hugging bohemian. I have friends who are artists, musicians, healers, shamans and circus performers, but I also have a few red lipstick wearing Republicans close to my heart (we just don't talk politics). I also like red lipstick on special occasions (all natural and purchased at Whole Foods).

Beyond the Sedona immersion, my daughter and I have gone to churches, full moon ceremonies, solstice events and prayerful dinner parties. Yesterday we went to Good Will and scored a perfectly fitting kimono. My daughter wanted to stay up late and dance under the stars in it, not a school night … so that's what we did (for about five minutes). As said earlier we read the Bible, we read about goddesses and make frequent requests to our Archangels for our well-being and for those close to us and well, the whole earth. Ask your children what they think and feel, ask them what a plant or animal is saying and take them to places where they can comfortably speak, about what they already know.

<u>**Your child seems "different" from what you know them to be:**</u> If your child seems "off" consider age-old remedies to restore. If you're an Italian, you might spit vodka in the four directions of your home. If you're a Native American you might light a white candle and grab

your sage bundle to move out those home particle memories (some people call them ghosts). If you are a modern day Shaman you might burn a little Palo Santo and rub fresh (must be fresh) basil across the forehead and wrists to clear the aura. If you are a Catholic you might put a scapular on the crib (or co-sleep) then bless the forehead, heart and shoulders with holy water. If you are from India, maybe apply some kohl under the eyes and make a firm dedication to Durga, who will burn away demons. Don't lose ritual, people of all races, and in all time, have been clearing energy. They were not stupid, they were right on. Please don't be a modern-day skeptic; pick a path and help your child clear energy, they are sometimes inundated. As for myself and daughter, we pray the 23rd psalm, call for the angelic, light a white candle and burn sage, sometimes Palo Santo or run a bath with salt and basil. Also a quick Hail Mary is super helpful as the Blessed Mother is practically universal in her calming. **Note:** Prior to psychotherapy, rituals as said above (along with many other cultural or spiritual means not named here) are how personality disruptions in childhood were handled. I think we should never throw the baby out with the bath water (this is metaphorical, please no throwing baby anywhere until they are ten and into a pool and they can swim). **Double note:** Everything has energy. Prayer and rituals come with an intention/directed energy to preserve divinity. Science and spirituality are the same.

Buddha story: My daughter and I were staying at my dearest friends' house Deb and Lisa (thank you for all the love and care-giving you have given us), temporarily, in one of those frequent move transitions. I placed my approximately 24 inch Buddha statue outside of their home close to a large round bush. This bush (as said by Deb and Lisa) always grew only large and round. In the six weeks we were with them, one branch of the bush grew strait out to the left (maybe 3ft long) like an arm, directly in front of the Buddha statue. Deb and Lisa, who are a lot more practical about circumstances than I am, were amazed (because there was inarguably some sort of divinity going on here). *I believe that God is the divine force of nature (or instinct ... GUT, hint, hint, now apply all earlier Gut + Research equations more deeply) that told elephants to seek higher ground before a devastating tsunami hit in 2004. Elephants have more glial cells than we do and frankly, they are less distracted so as to connect to that divine force (no cell phones and soccer games)! That same divine force comes with your child. Keep it on, in any way you are comfortable with.*

PART II: EMOTIONS AND HEALING THEM

1. SLEEP, CHALLENGE and STRENGTH:

Parenting young children can be a super challenging time period and we might do well to think of it as an incredible experience. Like climbing Mt. Everest, you have to stay strong and focused, exhibit extraordinary endurance and love with passion the dream of reaching your goal. Your goal could be as simple as loving the moment, no matter what that moment is. I have spoken with countless mothers who feel like a failure, because in our culture parenthood is "supposed to be the best time of your life." Uh, it's not, it's when you were twenty, on a plane to Paris to backpack through Europe with five of your best friends. Anyway, this parenting-best-time-of-your-life pretense can cause great isolation for mothers, who think their peers are somehow having an easier time of it, blissfully enjoying their babies. I have met families like this, but they tend to be rare (and possibly giving us a snow job). Most families when you get down to it, deeply love their children and are also deeply, challenged.

Sleep deprivation and a complete change in one's personal drives (satisfying one's own needs verses the constant demand of another), can feel like a psychological crisis. It is temporary. You won't be climbing Mt. Everest forever and of course, it's also dependent on the disposition of your children, how many you have and so on. It's not a bad time to find religion, spirituality or a devotion to a Guru, prayer in the middle of the night helps.

Mother and father warriors: As you know, in part of my daughter's infancy, I lived in Sedona, Arizona. I was getting up nightly with my daughter and it was really, really hard. While there (in Sedona), I met an interesting man on a very interesting "Spiritual Warrior" path. Those practicing this discipline, purposely wake themselves at two a.m., and stay up until morning, sleeping four hours each night over the course of one year. The philosophy of this practice states that, if you can master your emotions when you're sleep deprived, you can master them anytime. Whoever created this discipline would have called me aside and said, "Look I think you are nice person, but you just don't have what it takes, maybe take up tennis and read the bible instead." Except that we, as parents, can't just stop the practice, our babies are crying! Anyway, this very, disciplined gentleman said that all mothers are spiritual warriors. I agree with this and, would like to add, fathers, too. Unless you are a 1950s type dad who peacefully sleeps through your child's infancy, well then, no spiritual warrior medal for you … and dude, I am sure that you are a lovely man, but get your ass out of bed and give your lady a break.

Side note: It is not necessarily a great time to evaluate your marriage or couple status when raising infants and toddlers. It's like trying to take a census with a tornado coming through your town. Just get in the basement and hide out until it's over. I know, I know … I've been divorced twice, how could I possibly give advice on this topic. You make an excellent point … and still I proceed. Tension is absolutely inevitable because the two of you are likely vying for personal time and if one of you gets a little more of it, someone might be hatin' on the other. Make a schedule … his personal time and her personal time (or her/her or him/him personal time), along with home dating. Then after that, dig deep. Find your love. Breathe and when your children are over the age of five or six, come out of the basement and look at each other again. You have another six or seven years, before the teenage years. I am sure that in the future medical marijuana will be issued for parents of toddlers and teenagers. Anyway, hang tight, tough phases end.

Gratitude eases parenthood: Sleep deprivation may be short in the scheme of things, but there are other sorts of emotional and behavioral issues that accompany parenthood long-term. Slow down and breathe, or go outside for a minute and use awful curse words. Well, maybe go outside and put your bare feet on the ground, with more breathing ... and then, just a few awful curse words. Whatever you choose, just get back in the game. Don't be a harsh judge of self. Keep that self as happy as possible. When your child falls asleep, whisper in their ear about how grateful you are for them, no matter how you feel in that moment or how crappy you feel about the day. Gratitude erases the resentment you will undoubtedly feel at times, for being pushed to your physical limits. Tell yourself, "I chose this child, I chose this challenge in some way" and "I know I can do it" and "I am bigger and stronger because of this" and "I am so grateful for this life." There is no dissonant pattern that will stick between you and your child, when gratitude is exercised. "I am so grateful for you" goes a very, very, long way.

Search Item: The power of gratitude.

2. THE AMYGDALA GLAND ON HIGH ALERT:

So now that we have got you all grateful even though you are not sleeping regularly, now we need to turn off the stress cycle. The amygdala gland is part of our emotional memory within the limbic system, located behind the eyes, in the lower center of our brain (www.benbest.com/science/anatmind/anatmd9.html). It is the molecular storehouse of our life's emotions and in part, our parents' emotions, their parents' emotions and so on (Debiec, J and Sullivan RM, 2014). It is a function of our "fight or flight" response, and when this gland opens in response to stress, it sets in motion, the release of stress chemicals (health.harvard.edu/staying-healthy/understanding-the-stress-response). **Side note:** Much of my first understanding of the amygdala gland came from the teachings of Dr. Julian Ford, professor at the University of Connecticut. While working at a clinic in Connecticut (in 2010), I learned aspects of a treatment model he created called TARGET Trauma Affect Regulation: Guide for Education and Therapy. In the model, Dr. Ford teaches a person to close the amygdala gland in an effort to turn off the fight or flight response. The following segments are, in part, inspired by his teachings as was the creation of my brain reprogramming treatment detailed in the coming section. I even talked to him on the phone a couple of times telling him about my glial cell stuff. Oh … he has a book, *Hijacked by Your Brain: How to Free Yourself When Stress Takes Over*. If times are tough for you (I am so sorry), maybe just switch to his book. Thank you Dr. Ford!

Baby cries, amygdala gland opens, old emotions: I theorize that repressed emotions can become opened in you during the first year of your child's life and through their development. Biologically, your central nervous system can be put into urgency mode, because of the crying and waking cycles of a new baby. So, you're not sleeping normally. Your central nervous system is regularly in alarm mode due to your baby's cries to have its needs met (or due to the demands of young children). Because the amygdala gland is the storehouse of emotions, I theorize that when it's opening (such as with baby crying, exhaustion and so forth) your repressed emotions and memories now have a chance to surface. Those repressed emotions can rear their very uncomfortable and possibly painful head at a time, when you could use a break, rather than a therapy session, with your infant. So what do you do? Orient yourself to the present. Go to a window or go outside. Get with a tree. Tell the amygdala gland to close! If it's your thing to pray, it's a good time for it. Identify the emotions, identify the thoughts you're thinking. Then dissolve it (see section below on programming the brain). Say out loud that you're feeling a good feeling, even when you're not. Your glial cells will listen to the negative or the positive, choose the positive so that your brain can produce chemical messages of well-being and your body can move toward calm at a faster rate.

Remember, emotions can make a miserable thought, and a miserable thought, creates more miserable emotion. If you say, "I feel calm and everything is alright," the glial cells are directed to slow the brain and body down once again. If you say, "This is awful, we are out of control" and so on, the glial cells inform the brain and body that there is still an emergency, and therefore, more stress chemicals flow. This requires a lot of diligence, because negative emotions can be seductive. You are stronger than the seduction! Stay aware, be the observer of your brain and support yourself in whatever way heals you. If you need to get outside help, be it priest, shaman, therapist or from a very, unprepared neighbor who finds you crying at their door, don't be afraid to go get it. We all need support. You are not alone in this!

Please write this down then post on your fridge …

What will I choose today?

A. (stress thoughts = stress chemicals = anxious feelings = more stress thoughts = more stress chemicals = more anxious feelings = repeat)

B. (calm thoughts = calm chemicals = calm feelings = more calm thoughts = more calm chemicals = more calm feelings = repeat)

3. YOUR EARLY CHILDHOOD/LIFE HISTORY UN-REPRESSED:

There is hardly a more challenging role (and rewarding! and greatest love of your life!) in the world than being the mother or primary caregiver of a child under the age of three, unless you have more than one, under the age of three. My mother, at age 24, had a two year old, one year old and me, the newborn. You can imagine the exhaustion, desperation and agonizing stress. This seemingly impossible task of changing diapers, feeding in the middle of the night and crying in endless cycles could break an enemy of war. Spies would volunteer their top secret information just to get a night's sleep, probably choosing a holding cell, over the three baby, diaper-change, feed, no sleep, crying scenario.

So let's be real here, my mother has the strength of an elephant and my father, an ox. My father may have been slightly luckier, because he got to leave the house and work every day. Not luckier by much … he was still working all day, then feeding, bathing, diaper changing, etc. However, I do want to say, if you are the working parent, you possibly have it easier. So don't get down on your stay-at-home, baby mama or stay-at-home, baby daddy, they are standing in the thick of deep emotion all day long, with their amygdala gland wide open, flashing them a cascade of repressed emotion. You are at work, with a closed amygdala gland, sometimes getting a coffee break and going to the bathroom by yourself. So when you get home, pull out your wallet, give them all the money you have, and then say, "Thank you so much for all your hard work today" and "What can I do to help you?" And with hope, your partner turns to you, gives you a kiss and says, "I'll just take half the money, sweetie, and please, just let me sleep."

With all that said, I had these really grand visions of being the best mother a newborn baby girl could hope for (as you can probably tell, I have a lot of idealistic viewpoints). Well, that was not exactly the case, but I loved this little being so fiercely, I was ready to take out an elementary school kid just for using rude words in front of her. Despite my aims for perfection, I had an enormous amount of repressed and unresolved issues (who doesn't?) So, along with being joyful, enamored, and adoring, I was also feeling anxiety, nervousness, desperation, sorrow, overwhelmed, anger and hopelessness, just to name a few. Not all the time, but in reaction to sleeplessness and the central nervous system overload from baby crying and toddler whining or tantrums. The feelings were well-beyond what I know to be typically true of myself, perhaps this is the diagnosis of postpartum depression or, the blight of all mothers (and possibly fathers), in varying degrees. So what's the deal? What's happening?

Generations repeat patterns of parent challenge: As said in the previous section, when a baby cries, it can trigger the fight or flight response and possibly the opening of the amygdala gland in the parent. Not just from babies crying, young children are very easily upset, regularly triggering us as well. This interplay of child emotion now mixes with the repressed emotions of both parents and the memories/emotions of generations past, in a dramatic exchange of repeating patterns. Two year-olds likely become insistent to evolve themselves from all the history of human turmoil, they are sloshing around in. ***** In an article titled *Intergenerational transmission of emotional trauma through amygdala-dependent mother-to-infant transfer of specific fear*, it indicates that an infant gets an imprint of fears through parent cues in a process that is followed to a degree from one generation to the next (2014).

I now understand, that I was feeling my early childhood in replay, and my mother had been feeling, her early childhood in replay, except with three babies (which later becomes four children ... my younger brother). Take a moment of silence now for parents of multiple children, they could run the world. Anyway, that's a ton of emotion. So now my mother and father's ton of emotion that they had during my early childhood is opened up in me, along with my grandparent's and my great grandparent's and so on. Essentially, my baby was crying, and I was feeling generations of challenged mothers and fathers (along with all the unresolved challenges in my own life history). Basically, the infant brain imprints the feelings of their parents who are likely challenged in some way. When that infant grown to adult has their own children, there is the current challenge of parenting, along with the imprinted history.

Search Item: Check out www.theatlantic.com/health/archive/2015/01/what-happens-to-a-womans-brain-when-she-becomes-a-mother/384179/.

Stress chemicals and DNA: When the amygdala gland opens and stress chemicals flow, activated astrocytes could turn on DNA codes in you associated with anger, depression, anxiety and so on. I theorize that DNA codes passed from a few generations back could be sourcing that anger, depression, anxiety and so on, possibly igniting the typical day to day to feel more intense (see coming section on programming the brain as a possible solution).

*****I would now like to specially thank my mother and father for their dedication to me and to my siblings. My father always said that the job of each generation is to make the next one better. My parents have worked very, very, very hard, to make that true and they have never stopped evolving.

4. SELF PROGRAM THE BRAIN:

I am typically an obscenely optimistic person … this ship is going down and I am saying, "these big waves are so fun." I've always believed that I could change my life by changing my thinking. I have witnessed miracles made by my positivism. Not to say, that I was leading a life that most people thought was perfect. Mostly, they thought that I was living the life of some economically challenged, free spirit. They probably wanted to say or said in their heads, "Kate, get real, you have no money and poetry and art are for the eccentric." At the time (2001 to present), I had intermittent reprieves from social work for spiritual growth, travel, writing, researching and painting. In any case, this type of living put me to the edge often, where I had to think myself into a solution.

Because I had no health care for a while, solving my health issues (which thankfully, had been minor) was up to my creativity as well. In my exploration of the spiritual, metaphysics and holistic health, I learned that I could visualize myself well and it would work. This power of the mind to make change got me to wondering how it was all working scientifically and biologically, hence all those years of independent research on the glial cells. Parenting, evolving through parenting and some years of personal high stress/trauma, was how I really learned about how one can activate a physical response, by directing the glial cells. When I was feeling those intense emotions, post my daughter's birth and into her early years, I began directing the glial cells to dissolve those intense thoughts/feelings, then replacing the brain connections of good thought. I found that my mood would change or that I could pass through a cold quickly or even manifest a check in the mail.

SPECIAL NOTE: It is important to note that people give up on optimism and positive thinking, because it is competing with memories, life and family history. It is therefore, of high importance to dissolve, trash and burn up the old, so that the new thought and direction has a chance to move. Remember everything is energy … thanks Einstein!!! Also, the dissolving and replacing doesn't complete, it is an ongoing process that brings strength and improvement. There are still difficult moments that are hopefully shorter and less painful. Don't give in to negative emotion, it probably just means a frustrating situation has tapped into or opened up a bunch of memory files. Direct the brain to close the files. Dissolve the negative emotion then move on to positive thought and action. You may have to do this in an ongoing way throughout the day. It gets better! Don't give up or give in! We are in this together!

*****My clients who use the reprogramming more regularly and can observe their brain processes rather than become the memory or emotion, progress in a faster way in both their inside (thoughts and emotions) and outside world (life around them).

Neuroscientists think you can brain reprogram: So somewhere in 2011, I created a brain reprogramming therapy, called Self Programming of Glia (SPG), and, as you already know, attempt to pitch it (for the next five or so years), for the purposes of research, with doctors in lots of places like Yale Prevention Research Center, Yale Cancer Center and other Connecticut hospitals (with mostly, very good support but no research study to fruition). Most recently, I have been working with a UCONN Neuroscientist on a research protocol using SPG with persons who are diagnosed with fibromyalgia. I was even given an associate professor position at UCONN because we had confidence that a grant would come through. However, we have three times gone for a grant and we have yet to receive money. These things take time or as I have often found out (sometimes the hard and painful way), there is another path that I have not yet seen. I am grateful for the one path here with you. Though I will say, it is very encouraging that some doctors and neuroscientists believe that our thought can direct the other 90% of our brains!!! We can! really tell those beautiful puffs of calcium waves in our astrocytes how you want to feel and how you want your body to work. Repeating thoughts make repeated communication and connections via these cells. **Note:** If you talk to your regular doctor about this they might look at you a little funny, but, if you have a neuroscientist friend, they will hopefully say, "makes sense to me." Well, unless your friend is the neuroscientist from California that I spoke to five years back, who said something to the feeling of, "You are a stupid social worker, what do you know?" I am sure he spends his Friday nights with his neuroscientist friends drinking tall green tea lattes, while discussing how important neurons are to the function of the brain … and while green tea lattes are delicious, and neurons are super awesome, it's glial cells, baby!, that command the ship!

*****The placebo effect has been a mystery forever. I bring up the hypothesis about the placebo effect from section 1, because I want to emphasize how belief (or what you tell your brain) can change physiology or an emotional state of being (via the glial cells as is my theory). The sugar pill is ingested (associated with belief) thereby providing glial cells a direction and call for action. I theorize that if glial cells don't have enough of what they need, they could always morph some stem cells into astrocytes or they can replicate themselves … astrocytes make astrocytes or astrocytes make neurons, so that the belief or glial cell direction can be accomplished.

SPG is a brain reprogramming treatment, not unlike cognitive therapy, which pulls out memory files or patterns of thinking and reshapes them through neuroplasticity. In SPG treatment, there is an understanding that a cognitive change is a biological directive to the glial cells. I now use SPG, with my clients in my private practice, with my daughter and with myself (and probably anyone who will listen to me). Clients who I have worked with have reported improved mood, improved relationships, improved connection to self and improved physical health. In the subsequent section, I give information about SPG because I hope it will help you to clean out those repressed emotions and history (which are now just particles in the brain … not big scary events still happening). With that said, I still sometimes feel scared of my particle history, but the more you reprogram the faster and easier it gets. **Note:** If you clean for yourself, you clean for your children. **Double Note:** SPG is not just for past emotions, but for current ones as well!

Here's how it works. Let's say you are feeling desperation on any given day, the nap never happened, the crying was close to constant, and you want to throw a piece a furniture out the window, just to release some tension. Instead, you can reprogram the glial cells to get yourself feeling better. (This will save your furniture and keep the neighbors from thinking you have a few screws loose.) **Note:** SPG is not for robots who never feel anything. Life is happening and sometimes you have to face and feel it then move yourself into a better state.

Self Programming of Glia (SPG) uses three prescription statements (thoughts repeated to reprogram the brain).

The **first statement** is a reprogram of the negative neruo-connections. A statement could be … "I have dissolved all feelings of desperation and accompanying thoughts, from my memory centers and central nervous system." Instead of saying over and over, "this is awful, I feel terrible, things are never going to get better," you are turning and facing the feeling, then dissolving it. In actuality, you are dissolving brain connections that support depressed thought or other unwanted neuro-structures.

*****In working daily on self (should you choose), you are looking for and deleting old or negative neuro-connections sourced from:

1.) Life events
2.) Negative thinking patterns/negative self-concept ideas
3.) Challenging emotions

The **second statement** is created to tell the glial cells how you want the brain and body to function, what you want to do and how you want to feel, something like "I have a balanced release of neurotransmitters. I feel calm and well. I have restored feelings of strength, joy and love."

After you have found the life event, negative thinking pattern or emotion, reconnect its opposite and go ahead on with your good life! Push the notion you want for yourself, until it fully connects in the neuro-system! Never give up or turn back!

The **third statement** is always the same, "I am self-healed by programming my glial cells." Basically, this last statement is to program the brain to program itself. No one really says, "Oh, by the way, you can biologically program the functions of your brain and body and please do so." Essentially, this statement is about belief. Like a good placebo pill, belief makes physiological change so I theorize.

Remember the reprogram includes three steps:

1.) Dissolve
2.) Recreate/Restore
3.) Actualize Programming.

Here's some examples …

Perhaps, one of your parents passed away a few years back (I am very sorry if this is true). As that amygdala gland is opening, due to normal baby/child demands, you might be tapping into that loss and possibly unhealed grief. This could lead to depressed feelings, beyond typical.

You might use statements like...
  1.) I have dissolved all grief about the loss of my father, from my amygdala gland and

central nervous system.

2.) My amygdala gland is closed. My astrocytes are in their resting state, where I feel calm, balanced and peaceful. I now feel connected to my father by loving feelings and loving memories.

3.) I am self-healed by programming my glial cells.

Maybe you're feeling intense anxiety. You recognize that your mother was under incredible financial and emotional strain when you were born. Because the amygdala gland is opening regularly in you, you are not only feeling the strain of your current life, but possibly your mother's strain imprinted in your emotional memory center from your early childhood.

Statements could be ...

1.) I have dissolved all my anxiety, and my mother's anxiety, from my memory centers and central nervous system.

2.) My amygdala gland is closed. My astrocytes are in their resting state. Everything is going to be fine. I have everything I need. I feel strong and centered.

3.) I am self-healed by programming my glial cells.

Perhaps you feel anger, unsure of the cause. You can use the statements ...

1.) I have dissolved feelings of anger from my brain and body, at the root cause from my memory centers and central nervous system.

2.) My astrocytes are in their resting state, where everything feels comfortable and relaxed. I feel calm and well-adjusted.

3.) I am self-healed by programming my glial cells.

You can even create statements to say to your baby or child. Children are already sponges but if you speak to them while they are sleeping, words and concepts go into the brain faster, because they are unhampered by the activity of the frontal lobe. You can say things for them, like, "I sleep well all through the night" or "I am well-adjusted, loved and happy." You can also dissolve negative emotions that they might be feeling from you, saying for them, "I have dissolved Mommy's anxiety" and "I replace that feeling with calm, comfort and security." **Note:** Because of the extra absorbent mind of a sleeping child, please be sure not to argue or use harsh words or watch violent television in the presence of your sleeping child (if you can).

If you can become the observer of the brain, you are far less likely to be seduced into negative emotion, and thereby negative thought, and, therefore, more negative emotion. If you label it, "Oh, that's hopelessness" and identify the cause, "Where is it coming from?" and then, dissolve and replace it, it will be easier to stay strong. This will help you to live in the moment with your children, rather than from continuous negative memory. *****Most ongoing suffering comes from memory.** You are a rushing river! When you hit a file, don't open it and explore the concepts, just identify it and keep it closed. Delete the emotions connected to it and stay on the river. The bad feeling will be gone in minutes, the past is not happening now! **Note:** If you are in the middle of a crisis, you may need outside support such as a therapist and may need to take action to resolve the circumstance. Please get what you need for the moment. Also, if there are big issues that have never been processed, I am not suggesting that you skip the facing part of difficult scenarios (maybe see a therapist or other type of healer/professional). Then ... after you've faced it or the crisis has resolved, get the hell out of there, close it and set it to flames. You got a lot of livin' to do!

I have included a list of statements that address a variety of issues that can surface as a new parent, in the process of parenthood and, frankly, in being a human. Please use them to free your mind of old memory and give space for new feelings and thoughts that support a reality of current happiness. The more you clean past memory, the more joy you will feel. Remember the past is just a bunch of dirty particles in the brain.

Your parents' stress during your childhood: When you are an embryo, infant and young child, you are, essentially absorbing your parents' feelings and experiences into the developing memory centers of the brain. It can later become your fears, hang-ups or strengths, depending upon your circumstance and disposition. There is no blame to the previous generation they are evolving from the one before them, which likely had even more intense issues. We are all a part of advancing human biology in the best way we can. I hope this helps to change ill-patterns in a faster, less painful way. The first category is …

Your parents' feelings and experiences (because they could have imprinted in your early childhood developing brain):

The first statement is, "I have dissolved all emotions, feelings and memories from my brain and body regarding (whatever applies to you) ..."

My parents' arguments about finances
My parents' arguments with each other
My parents' stress about housing or frequent moving
My parents' stress about employment
My parents' difficult adjustment to parenting
My parents' separation and divorce
My parents' history of their own trauma surfacing in my childhood
My parents' stress about household cleanliness
My parents' stress about sleep deprivation
My parents' life traumas (parent life traumas are passed down, so if you know of them, please dissolve them in you)
My parents' anxiety
My parents low self-worth

Alright so, after you have dissolved the memories that apply to you, the second step is to create/replace the brain connection that you want. For example, regarding a parents' stress about employment, you would simply change the feeling state inside you by saying, "I replace that stress with feelings of calm and stability. I am abundant. All is well." Please follow up with your third statement, which is …. "I am self-healed by programming my glial cells."

Generational gene codes could come from trauma?: In my work with clients, **I have come to theorize that generational trauma must make gene codes.** For example, a client fainted while she was working and later came to me because she subsequently developed anxiety and a fear of fainting. She also developed a repeating thought that she's trapped or that she will not be able to escape, when in certain situations. In doing some digging, we found that the client's mother is easily startled and somewhat claustrophobic, and then we found that her paternal grandfather was a prisoner of war during the Korean War. Now imagine what a prisoner of war thinks and feels … tremendous anxiety/terror, feeling trapped and can't escape. Maybe this becomes a gene code that gets passed to his daughter as mild claustrophobia, then the gene code is passed to his granddaughter (my client), but remains dormant. The code possibly gets tripped on by the fainting incident representing itself as intense anxiety (which she never had, in fact she had a stellar life history and comes from a very good family experience). Here's a plug for prescription statements addressing gene codes … this client reported some improvement using statements to deprogram anxiety and program calm. However … she reported the greatest improvement when she used a deprogramming statement to silence gene codes related to her grandfather's war trauma and a reprogramming statement to restore healthy genetic expression of calm. **Note:** I have also found that my clients who have fibromyalgia (less than 10 clients with said condition) have a grandfather or great grandfather who served in World War II. More research is needed about how trauma mutates gene codes. Whatever history that you know about, dissolve it, because it is likely somewhere in you. Remember stress and trauma can flip on these codes, so let's get rid of old history in the form of faulty DNA codes, before they ever have a chance to flip on. Your astrocytes are amazing and I believe that they will get the job done through programming them!

Next categories ….

Childhood Experiences:

*****The above categories relate to your parent's experiences imprinting upon you, the next categories are related to your direct experiences.

I have dissolved the emotions, brain connections and trauma, from my central nervous system and memory centers regarding:

Birth trauma (everyone should say a statement around this just in case)
Trauma of circumcision
Trauma of vaccination
Lack of bond with primary caregiver
Infant or childhood illness
Sleep difficulties
Neglect
Accident/injury
Separation from a parent
Colic or frequent crying as an infant (difficulty being consoled)
Head trauma
Hospitalization of a parent
Death of a parent or close loved one
Teasing by relative

Difficulty separating from a parent or difficult transitioning to school
Embarrassment by teacher
Difficulty completing school work or meeting school standards
Loss of self-direction, due to imposed adult/school value
Frequent family conflicts
Parent's mental illness
Parent's anxiety or depression
Bullied at school or in the neighborhood
Difficulty making friends
Sibling arguments/fights
Parent's alcoholism or substance abuse
Domestic violence
Remorse for not meeting parent expectations
Parent's disappointment (in you) for not meeting expectations
Parent chaotic household/child loss of control
Parent's animosity toward child's demand
Parent blaming you for family problems
Parent's excessive worry
Parent's projection of a fearful event (worried that something in parent life history will happen to child)
Parent shaming
Parent lack of empathy to child feelings
Parent criticism

*****Everyone may need to dissolve parent/grandparent/great-grandparent shaming, because generations of human beings have used this emotion to control children's behavior. It is thick in our genetics. I have watched myself do this to my own daughter. It's awful and just comes out. There is so much diligence required to be sure that our consequences, boundaries and limits are coming from teaching, supporting and directing, rather than shaming. The deal is, kids require so much attention and sometimes you just feel pissed, and it gets personal, and this genetic bad parenting technique (shaming) springs into play. Together we can dissolve those shaming patterns for generations to come.

*****When you find the source of specific patterns that have defined your life especially in regards to self-worth and value, you will have to diligently reprogram. As memory files pop up related to that pattern (or other old files) delete and replace them like a computer inbox. Find the thinking patterns and emotions sourced from these life events … then more deleting, dissolving, replacing and restoring. There will be good days and bad days, don't give up!

Of course, the list could go on, but whatever you find, don't blame your parents, forgive them. They likely did the best they could, with what they had been given. When you recognize something, get mad, sad or cry for a minute if you need to, but then go on, make a new brain connection. Your child needs you now and needs you to do it differently. So, make the new connection, follow up with that replacement statement, such as "I feel strong. I am well-loved. I feel calm and well adjusted. Everything is OK. I am now stable." Or in the case of shaming, "I am a patient, strong and clear thinking parent, applying consequences and limits in the intention of love." Then ... "I am self-healed by programming my glial cells."

Childhood Abuse:

I have dissolved all traumatic memory and emotions, from my brain and body associated with:

Parent or relative emotional/verbal abuse
Parent or relative physical abuse
Parent or relative sexual abuse
Sibling abuse (of any kind)
Professional or neighbor abuse (of any kind)

Replacement statements here might be something like ... "My amygdala gland is closed. My astrocytes are in their resting state. I am strong, well-balanced, with good boundaries and a secure feeling. My body is in the present moment and is healed." Then ... "I am self-healed by programming my glial cells." ******Thinking patterns associated with abuse have loads to do with low self-value, please find them and delete/replace!

SPECIAL NOTE: *If you were not abused, but your parent was abused as a child, you may want to use the above statements because you likely carry particles of their trauma inside you. Further, you likely have ancestors that have been abused, which I believe is stored in our junk DNA. So if you are human, you may want to say the above statements regarding abuse.*

Work with a therapist: If there has been abuse issues of any kind, during your early childhood or otherwise, you will additionally want to consider work with a therapist, a hypnotherapist, or other type of practitioner, prior to being pregnant at best, or second best, during pregnancy, or third best, at any point in your child's development. Your child will show you, by irritating you, by agitating you or by igniting you, what you have left to heal. If you respond with irritation, agitation or by being ignited, you could inadvertently form similar patterns within your child. Stop it ahead of time, you really can. Separate from an abusive partner: If a partner is currently abusive to your child or to you, verbally, emotionally or otherwise, it must be stopped immediately. If your partner will not agree to a safety plan and treatment, there must be separation between the abusive partner and your children, in my opinion. Children need security and this trumps everything.

Life Traumas:

There are lots of circumstances that you walk through as a human being, and I am so sorry for the really tough ones you've experienced. It is important to clear out the trauma memory, especially the major ones. If you have already faced the issue or had treatment, you may be ready to move ahead. While the below situations can be very emotional and impacting, it is important to perceive them, as no longer existing. Your traumas are now faulty brain connections, causing negative emotion and negative thought. Change the connection. It will help you to be in the present moment.

I have dissolved all memory and emotions from my brain and body from:

Accidents/injuries
Divorce
Death of a loved one
Sexual trauma
Abusive relationships
History or using drugs
Alcoholism
Loss of employment
Relocation issues
Financial hardships
Cancer or other illness

Again, you will want to replace the negative experience in the biology of the brain and body. This can be achieved by saying something like "My amygdala gland is closed. My astrocytes are in their resting state. I have solid and secure relationships," or "I am healthy and full of life," or "I am financially abundant," etc. Then of course … "I am self-healed by programming my glial cells."

While I have not named, even close, to all possible traumas and life experiences, I hoped to give you a starting point in healing your history. If you, seriously get through and clean the life circumstances (and emotions connected to those events) in your biology, you will feel better and, it will be much less likely that your history, will play out in your child. Remember, what you say to your glial cells, is communicated to your child's glial cells via calcium waves. What is said inside the mind is said inside the mind of people next to you, and especially those closest to you. Thought waves travel. Travel beautiful ones!

*****I know there are lots of ways to heal the body … from doctor to therapist to shaman to brain reprogramming. I know there is God, science and religion. Underneath all of it is that divine force that we are subject to, like how the ocean cannot be argued about. In that force, is all the waves … water, light, thought, sound and love. Your glial cells have all of this.

5. PARENT/CHILD PATTERN EXCHANGING:

Habits and patterns: If you find yourself in a habit of aggravation with your child, be very aware, so you can employ different approaches. Again, when you are pushed so much physically (when they are babies) and emotionally (at every stage), intense feelings in you can sometimes create negative patterns between you and your child. I have had to undo a few, and if you are a human being, you'll be working on this like I am. Do the best you can. Give yourself, whatever it is, that brings you back to center. Use the above prescription statements, talk to a therapist, walk, meditate, pray or dance around your kitchen. Don't let the aggravation get to you. Pick yourself up. Dust yourself off. Remember the best of your child, and start again. You can do this! I know you can!

Children can act out our emotion: Not too long ago, my daughter woke in the middle of the night to go to the bathroom. Fine, but she walks like an elephant and then requires every need met, such as food, water, hugging, storytelling. Now I have been doing this sort of thing for 7 years in the middle of the night. Thank God, it is now very rare! I am actually not that nice anymore (in the middle of the night). I am more like, "If you don't stay completely still and go to sleep, you will never see the inside of a birthday party again!" Uh, this doesn't work. Please see a more skilled therapist for answers about this, I got nothing or so I thought. Then, after being up for two hours, a light bulb went on, at approximately 3:45 am!

Oh crap! I realize I've been resenting her for all of the times I've been up in unforgiving starlight. It's not that I logically resent her for our middle of the night escapades, she's a kid, this stuff happens, but I was illogically resenting her, simply because I JUST wanted to be sleeping. What dawned on me is that whatever emotion we have stuck in us, becomes a manifestation code in our children. My daughter, with a consciousness linked to mine, was in no uncertain terms awoken by my stored resentment of repeated all-nighters, no kegs or hot college boys. Our children, and people for that matter, can act out whatever template we have inside us, be it our wellness or our unrest. So, It was as if my daughter received a late night invitation (unbeknownst to me) to produce behaviors that supported the unchecked, ill-feeling inside me. What a job we have right?! Not only do we need to be basic need bitches ... I'm sorry, basic need mamas and papas as well as love, structure nurturers, but we also need to be keen scientific observers of our emotions and thoughts, so that our children don't unconsciously and theatrically perform them.

And so I got busy with the...

1.) I have dissolved "all resentment about being up in the middle of the night" from my memory centers and central nervous system.
2.) I restore the vibration of love and calm well-being. We sleep well all through the night. I love my daughter and I am so grateful for her.
3.) I am self-healed by programming my glial cells.

I ended that night by saying to my daughter, "No matter how frustrated I get, I am always on your team."

Parent/child Patterns: As you are cleaning out your own history (which as you know is ongoing, hopefully getting easier as you go) you can be cleaning patterns between you and your child. There are universal ones true to all parents or generationally inherited, such as shaming, frustration about repeating parent request and so on. Observe, then dissolve and replace.

The rarely told crazy parent syndrome: If you are pregnant, you need to hear this. If you have a child past four, you know what I'm talking about. You've seen that perfect looking family pull up in their BMW SUV (my dear friend has one, so no offense). Out comes blonde hair straightened wife with pink lipstick, just muscular enough husband and two dazzling children (I really have known great people like this, and love them!) Anyway, the kids are so respectful and thankful, talented and funny. The parents are so honoring and lovely. You have just freaked out on your runny nose, dirt-stained kid, saying things like, "All of your stuffed animals are mine, and you be will lucky to see them at your high school graduation." You can only imagine how these LL Beaners got down on one knee, while they patiently and gently told their congenial child, it's time to go now. You told your child fifteen times, kindly at first, until you've blown your top, making the definition of insanity – doing the same thing and expecting different results, true in your living room.

In the 1930s and 1940s, parents didn't have much time (or pressure) for feeling remorse about laying into their kid, there were wars and depressions going on. Children in the fifties and sixties, may have bypassed the lashings because of mother's little helper, better known as Valium, so not too much guilt there. The seventies children may have gotten a mix of old school discipline and a liberated marijuana mama, so maybe, not too much guilt there either. I am honestly not sure what happened in the eighties, it was more like a costume party, mothers in parachute pants and capezios, dancing with their kids to the first music videos? Somewhere in the nineties, I think we really started believing that what we said to our children in their early development really mattered. So now, when we blow up, we not only feel pissed off beyond belief, we launch into a massive guilt trip about how we damaged our child, and how the mother with the pink lipstick would feel, if she heard the tirade over putting shoes away. Then, it's onto feelings of failure and inadequacy. **Note:** I am mostly kidding about parents in history. I think we all deeply love our children and do the best we can in the context of our experience.

So, let's be real. The mother in the pink lipstick freaks out when she has to tell her son to do something fifteen times, and her son doesn't voluntarily pick up his toys or dirty clothes. As a therapist, I have come across all kinds, and I assure you, this parent-child experience is universal. We are all losing our tempers sometimes, and saying things at ugly, high-pitched tones that we would feel horrified about if our friends, neighbors or coworkers overheard. It doesn't mean we can justify our actions like some parents have done for countless generations, but it doesn't mean we should throw in the towel. Just use it to wipe off that touch of sweaty bitterness about asking a third time, frankly it just probably takes three times before it connects (hopefully getting better with age). You haven't failed and no one is doing it better than you. Well, maybe some, but mostly not. You still haven't failed.

I will say that there are lots of people doing it better than I am (please read their books). I have yelled and said ridiculous things in the heat of upset. My ideals were so high (as you may have noticed), that when I was standing knee deep in my unresolved emotions, playing out with my daughter, I was worried that I had ruined her. The truth is, if you have landed yourself a feisty being (usually one of your children does this for you), you have signed up for some soul-pushing, evolution-leaping sessions that make all the legs for progress, for you, for your child and for humanity. Yes, you need to heal. Yes, you need to correct bad parent behavior and yes, sometimes you need to yell, when you've had it. But ... you need to know, you are in this parenting thing, in part, to evolve yourself. Recognize this. You are not alone, you are transforming, and you know what, you are doing great things! So let that crappy moment go. Just seriously let it go. Your child will not become an ax murderer and, on really bad days, neither will you. **Note:** Be real with people about what it's like to be a parent, so they can tell you their story. When the hiding stops, we can all work together on solutions. I will tell you, that my heart has been broken, by how imperfect I am as a parent. And I will tell you that, my heart loves my daughter so deeply, and so we go on, forgiving the challenge of each day, evolving ourselves into a better moment.

6. CHEERS:

So much has been said in this book about possible choices to make along the way, about birthing and raising your child in the early years. It's up to you to decide, what makes the most sense, in the context of your environment. My hope is that you feel the inspiration to trust yourself and to trust the natural processes of birth, healing and living. I wish you the greatest of ease, and the greatest of blessings, on your journey as a parent and on your journey as a super, awesome individual. If your child is asleep, pour yourself a beautiful full glass of wine (preferably organic). It really is, another good day. If you're pregnant or nursing, the midwife (and doctor) said, you can have half a glass. I say just a touch more than half, wink, wink.

7. FUTURE THERAPY SESSION:

Well, I have decided that it is now time for me to publish this book and stop adding to it. My daughter knows that today is the day that we stop writing. She made a sign for us to post on a tree by the road which says … "My mom just finished a babby (baby) book. She wants all moms to be able to have it. So if your (you're) a mom whith (with) a new born babby (baby) call 860 xxx-xxxx ore (or) look on amazon." (Thank you honey, I love the sign and you immensely.) Anyway, thank you dear mothers and fathers. It was so nice to be with you and I hope we can talk again soon. In the coming months (into at least a year), I will write *The Little Book of Brain Reprogramming* which will read like a series of loving therapy sessions. So, maybe we can reconnect, talk some more and do all that inside work together. *Impact on Mermaid* will follow … sort of a big person's expanded version of *The Little Book of Baby/Child*. Keep your eye out for them please.

References:

1.) Abramowicz, JS, Kemkau, FW & Merz, E. (2012). *Obstectrical ultrasound: can the fetus hear the wave and feel the heat?* Ultraschall Med. June; 33(3):215-7.

2.) Alvarez, J., Katayama, T. and Prat, A. (2013). *Glial influence on the blood-brain barrier.* Glia vol. 61, issue 12, pages 1939-1958.

3.) Bartlett, Emily. (2013). *Are homepathic vaccines a good alternative to shots?* Retrieved from holisticsquid.com-homeopathic-vaccines-a-good-alternative.

4.) Bayarri, MJ, Rol de Lama MA, Madrid, JA, Sanchez FJ (2003). *Both pineal and lateral eyes are needed to sustain daily circulating melatonin rhythms in sea bass.* Brain Res 2003 April 18, 969 (1-2): 175-82.

5.) Castillo, M. (2010). *Stem cells, radial glial cells, and a unified origin of brain tumors,* doi: 10.3174/ajnr.A1674 AjNR201031: 389-390.

6.) Chopra, D. (1998). The Seven Spiritual Laws of Success. California: Amber-Allen Publishing

7.) Cornell-Bell AH, Finkbeiner SM, Cooper MS, Smith SJ. (1990). *Glutamate induces calcium waves in cultured astrocytes: long-range glial signaling.* Science. 247(4941):470-3.

8.) Debiec, J and Sullivan RM, (2014). *Intergenerational transmission of emotional trauma through amygdala-dependent mother-to-infant transfer of specific fear.* Proc Nati Acad Sci 2014 Aug 19, 111(33): 12222-7.

9.) Durairaj, L, Launspach, J., Watt, JL, Businga, TR, Kline, JN, Thorne, PS and Zabiner, J. (2004). Safety assessment of inhaled xylitol in mice and healthy volunteers. Respir Res. 2004 Sep 16, 5-13.

10.) Emoto, Masaru (2004). The Hidden Messages in Water. Tokyo, Japan: Sunmark Publishing.

11.) Fields, Douglas (2010). The Other Brain. New York: Simon & Schuster.

12.) Goldman, GS and Miller, NZ (2012). *Relative trends in hospitalizations and mortality among infants by the number of vaccine doses and age, based on the Vaccine Adverse Event Reporting System (VAERS), 1990-2010.* Hum Exp Toxicol Oct vol. 31.

13.) Gosselin, R., Suter, M., Ru-Rong, Ji, Descoterd, I. (2010). *Glial cells and chronic pain.* Neuroscientist October 2010 vol. 16 no 5 519-513.

14.) Han, X., Chen, M., Fushun W., Windrem M., Wang S., Shanz S., Xu Q et al. (2013). *Forebrain engraftment by human glial progenitor cells enhances synaptic plasticity and learning in adult mice.* Cell Stem Cell 2013 vol. 12, issue 3, p. 342-353, March.

15.) Heimer, M. (2013). *Routine Ultrasound Testing Not Proven Safe for Pregnant Women* retrieved from www.naturalnews.com/038833_ultrasound_pregnant_women_testing

16.) Hines DJ and Haydon PG (2014). *Astrocytic adenosine: from synapses to psychiatric disorders.* Philos Trans R Soc Lond B Biol Sci. 2014 Oct 19;369(1654):20130594.

17.) Lee, H., Ghetti, A., Pinto-Duarte, A., Wang, X., Dziewczapolski, G., Galimi, F., Resendiz, S., Pina-Crespo, J., Roberts, A., Verma, I., Sejnowski, T and Heinemann, S. (2014). *Astrocytes contribute to gamma oscillations and recognition memory.* Proceedings of the National Academy of Sciences. Retrieved from www.salk.edu.

18.) Huber, R., Treyer V., Borbely, AA., Schuderer J., Gottselig, J.M., Landolt, H.P., Werth, E., Berthold, T., Kuster, N., Buck, A., Achermann, P. (2002). *Electromagnetic Fields, such as those from mobile phones, alter regional cerebral blood flow in sleep and waking EEG.* J Sleep Res. 2002 Dec;11(4):289-95.

19.) Koob, A. (2009) The Root of Thought. Pearson Education, Upper Saddle River, New Jersey.

20.) Lieberman, E., O'Donoghue, C. (2002) Obstet Gynecol. Unintended effects of epidural analgesia during labor: a systematic review. May;186(5 Suppl Nature):S31-68.

21.) Mohney, Gillian (2013) New Birthing Trend, Don't Cut the Cord. Retrieved from abcnew.go.com/blogs/health/2013/04/11new-birthing-trend-don't-cut-the-cord/

22.) McKenna, J. and McDade, T. (2005) Why Babies Should Never Sleep Alone: A Review of the Co-Sleeping Controversy in Relation to SIDS, Bedsharing and Breast Feeding. Pediatric Respiratory Reviews (2005) 6, 34-52

23.) Mercer, JS, Erickson-Owens, DA. (2012). Rethinking placental transfusion and cord clamping issues. Perinat Neonatal Nurs. 2012 Jul-Sep;26(3):202-17; quiz 218-9. doi: 10.1097/JPN.0b013e31825d2d9a.

24.) Miller, D., *A User Friendly Vaccine Schedule.* Retrieved from https://www.lewrockwell.com/2004/12/donald-w-miller-jr-md/vaccine-nation Retrieved from pediatrics.about.com/od/immunizations/a/live-vaccines.htm.

25.) Pert, C. (1999). Molecules of Emotion. Touchstone. New York, NY.

26.) Readnower, RD, Chavko, M., Adeeb, S., Conroy MD, Pauly, JR, McCarron, RM and Sullivan, PG (2010). Increase in Blood-brain Barrier Permeability, Oxidative Stress, and Activated Microglia in a Rat Model of Blast-induced Traumatic Brain Injury. JNerosci Res, Dec. 88(16)3530-9.

27.) Saunders, N., Liddelow, S. and Dzieglielewska (2012). Barrier Mechanisms in the Developing Brain. Neurotoxicology. 2012 Jun;33(3):586-604. doi: 10.1016/j.neuro.2011.12.009.

Epub 2011 Dec 19

28.) Toljenovic, L and Shaw, CA (2011). Do Aluminum Vaccine Adjuvants Contribute to the Rising Prevalence of Autism? J Inorg Biochem 2011 Nov. 105)11): 1489-99.

29.) Trueba, G et al. (2000) Alternative Strategy to Decrease Cesarean Section: Support by Doulas During Labor. J Perinat Educ. 2000 Spring 9(2): 8-13.

30.) Williams, PM, Fletcher, S. (2010). Health effects of prenatal radiation exposure. AM Family Physician. September 1;82 (5): 488-93.

31.) Yanangisawa, T., Miake Y. Saeki, Y. and Takahashi, M. (2003). Remineralization effects of xylitol on demineralized enamel. J Electron Microscope (Tokyo) 2003; 52(5): 471-6.

32.) Zhao, T., Zou, S. and Knapp, P. (2009). Exposure to Cell Phone Radiation Up-Up-Regulates Apoptosis Genes in Primary Cultures of Neurons and Astrocytes. Neurosci Lett. Author manuscript; available in PMC Jul 20, 2009.

Online Sites Referenced:

1.) www.alternamoms.com On the "Safety and Usefulness of Prenatal Ultrasound"

2.) www.opednews.com/articles/American-Academy-of-Pediat-by-Dennis-Kucinich-121213-724.html)

3.)www.americanpregnancy.org/labornbirth/epidural

4.) www.biofortified.org/2013/11/answer-to-a-question-at-the-gmo-answers-website-will-gmo-wheat-silence-human-genes/

5.) www.babyreference.com/bonding-matters-the-chemistry-of-attachment/

6.)www.benbest.com/science/anatmind/anatmd9.html

7.) www.drkaslow.com/html/gluten-brain_connection_.htm.

8.) www.evidencebasedbirth.com (May 2012 *What is the Evidence for Pitocin Augmentation?*

9.) www.health.harvard.edu/staying-healthy/understanding-the-stress-response

10.) www.lewrockwell.com.

11.) www.livescience.com/21400-what-is-thehiggs-boson-god-particle-explained.html

12.) www.motherjones.com/blue-marble/2012/06/can-exposure-toxins-change-your-dna

13.) www.nih.gov/news-events/news-releases/gene-scan-shows-bodys-clock-influences-numerous-physical-functions

14.) www.mercolo.com

15.) www.medicinenet.com/circumcision

16.)www.nature.comneuro/journal/v6/n11/full/nn144.html

17.) www.natural-health-information-centre.com/sodium-lauryl-sulfate.html#ixzz3KmMTqUNN
Sodium Laureth Sulfate (SLES).

18.) www.nvic.org National Vaccine Information Center

19.) www.parentmap.com/article/babys-fourth-trimester-helping-your-baby-make-a-peaceful-transition-from-womb-to-world

20.) www.publicheatlthalert.org/mycoplasma--oftenoverlooked-in-chronic-lyme-disease.html

21.)www.wholesomebabyfood.momtastic.com/organics*for*homemadebabyfood.*htm*

22.) www.wisegeek.com/*what-are-the*-benefits-*of*-coconut-oil-for-babies

23.) www.womenofgrace.com/blog/?p=16584